She felt herself fading.

A scream welled up, but she couldn't get out even a sound. Terror flooded her.

Abruptly, the pressure eased and she fell, hitting her head on the corner of the sink. She was conscious enough to register a series of grunts and then a sickening thud against the tile.

Suddenly, Griffin was on the floor beside her.

"Laura?" He leaned over her, moving her hair gently out of her face as he peered at her. "Laura?"

His face came into focus, his hard-edged features stamped with concern.

She lifted a shaky hand to her throbbing head.

"Can you breathe?" he asked.

She nodded, forcing words past her bruised throat as she gripped his hand. "What happened?"

"You were attacked."

It had come too close on the heels of yesterday's attack. Fear sliced through her like a blade, jamming her breath painfully in her chest. "He found me. Vin found me."

"Looks that way."

Everything went black.

Debra Cowan, like many writers, made up stories in her head as a child. She planned to follow family tradition until she wrote her first novel. Equally inspired by Nancy Drew and fairy tales, she loves to combine suspense and romance in her novels. Debra lives in her native Oklahoma with her husband and enjoys hearing from readers. You can contact her via her website at debracowan.net.

Books by Debra Cowan

Love Inspired Suspense

Witness Undercover

Visit the Author Profile page at Harlequin.com for more titles

WITNESS UNDERCOVER

DEBRA COWAN

HARLEQUIN® LOVE INSPIRED® SUSPENSE

Recycling programs
for this product may
not exist in your area.

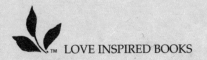 ™ LOVE INSPIRED BOOKS

ISBN-13: 978-0-373-67680-4

Witness Undercover

Copyright © 2015 by Debra S. Cowan

www.Harlequin.com

Printed in U.S.A.

Fear not, for I have redeemed you;
I have summoned you by name; you are mine.
–Isaiah 43:1

To the ladies of my Wednesday night Bible study—
Pennie, Stacy, Alison, Tami, Delise and Jane.
Thanks for the laughs and the prayers.

ONE

Laura Prentiss hadn't wanted a new beginning, a new name, but that was what she'd gotten. After the mess she'd made of her life, she was lucky to be alive.

Thanks to witness protection, she was now Laura Parker, assistant manager of Miss Behavin', a ladies' boutique in Pueblo, Colorado, that was currently closed for the night.

Thanksgiving was only weeks away. This would be her first here in Pueblo, her first without family. Laura tried not to feel sorry for herself.

She had a job and friends, even if they didn't know her real name. Jesus had left behind his family without complaining. She would be fine.

Just as she opened a case of potpourri to stock, she heard a knock on the back door.

Laura froze, her hands going clammy. It couldn't be a delivery, as it was after business hours. She reached for the bat in the corner kept for protection.

After her months in WitSec, had Vin Arrico finally found her?

The thought that her past might have caught up to her had Laura's stomach knotting. She crept to the door at the back of the storage room.

The knock sounded again, making her jump.

"Laura? Miss Parker?"

She recognized the thick Texas accent. "Marshal Yates?"

"Yes. I need to see you."

If the US marshal who had handled her case from the beginning had driven down from the field office in Colorado Springs, something was wrong. Very wrong.

Setting the bat aside, she unlocked the steel door and stepped back as the tall lanky man entered. He was followed by one of the biggest men Laura had ever seen. The stranger closed the door behind him, looking around at the shelves of candles, women's shoes and boxes of unpacked jewelry before shifting his attention to her.

Her shoulders tensed. In the light of the single-bulb fixture, she couldn't tell the color of his eyes, but they were piercing and glittered like steel. A strange sensation fluttered in her stomach. She turned to Floyd Yates.

"Has something happened with Vin?"

Laura had no doubt her ex-boyfriend could find her even from prison.

"No, nothing like that," Floyd said. "Sorry to alarm you."

He gestured to the man beside him. "Laura, this is Griffin Devaney."

She nodded at the stranger with neatly trimmed dark hair and whisker stubble. His six-foot-four frame filled the space. He studied her with a quiet certainty that made it difficult to breathe. Who was he? Why had Floyd brought him?

The open space seemed small and cramped with Griffin Devaney there. His well-fitting denim jacket was faded to a soft blue, as were his jeans.

The marshal turned to her. "Devaney works with your aunt at Enigma, Inc."

Laura started. Her aunt, Joy Langston, had worked at that company for years. Laura had never known how to label the enterprise. Private security? Personal security? Search and rescue?

Yates continued. "She sent Devaney for you and he contacted me."

Even though Laura knew she shouldn't have done so, she had told her aunt about WitSec the night she'd left Oklahoma City.

Joy knew Laura's situation, knew the danger posed by exposing her. So why had Floyd brought Devaney here?

Palms clammy, she clasped her hands together, her attention locked on the man who had protected her for the past ten months. "Just tell me."

"Your father has cancer," Floyd said. "A relapse of non-Hodgkin's lymphoma."

Relapse? Panic punched her in the chest followed quickly by resentment and regret. Her mother had died from cancer. Was her father close to death? Did he want to see her?

"He was first diagnosed nine months ago. He was cautioned that if the cancer returned, he would need a bone marrow transplant."

Devaney spoke up. "A lot of people have been tested, but you're the only match."

She frowned. "How do you know that?"

"You had a blood sample in the donor registry."

Before going into hiding, Laura had regularly donated blood and made sure to put herself on the register for both blood and bone marrow donors. She turned to Floyd. "You said my dad had relapsed."

"Yes. Two weeks ago, during his monthly check up, he learned the cancer was back."

Two bouts of cancer. A bone marrow transplant. Her guilt over their years-long estrangement pinched at her. Laura was the last person on earth her father would want to help him, but Floyd and Devaney didn't need to know that.

She glanced at the marshal. "Have you known about this since Dad's first diagnosis?"

"No." He hooked a thumb at the big man beside him. "Not until Devaney told me tonight."

Even if Floyd had known, it would've done no good to tell Laura. She wouldn't have been able to help her dad and her dad hadn't needed her then. But he did now.

"What about Vin?"

"My boss called to tell me that Devaney was coming. He's convinced this man can keep you safe. Devaney made a compelling case himself. He'll be with you 24/7 and he has backup if he needs it."

She could read nothing in the younger man's rugged features, the tight mouth or eyes that she could now see were a perfect mix of blue and green. There was a stillness about him yet also a hum of coiled energy beneath the surface, as if he could explode into motion faster than she could blink.

She drew in a deep breath. The everyday scents of perfume and potpourri and a light citrus cleaner were comforting. "I'm supposed to just disappear? Again?"

"I'm sorry, but yes," Floyd said gently. "I'll have your apartment packed up and your things sent to you when you're ready for them."

"I'll have to cancel my lease," she said, half to herself. "Are you sure my leaving witness protection is safe?"

"It's a risk. I won't lie. Nobody would blame you if you said no. If you say no, we can all just forget about this conversation."

"I can't do that," Laura said quickly. "Not if my dad really needs me."

"I think he does," the marshal said.

She trusted Floyd. He had never lied to her or put her in unnecessary danger.

She was going home. Aunt Joy needed her. Her father needed her. And then she would have to start all over again.

Having the marshal here and disappearing without notice meant her identity had now been compromised. After everything was done, she'd have to be moved, assigned another fake name and background. Get another job.

Sadness tugged at her. She'd made friends here and she really liked the store's owner, Ann Childress, but Laura had never let herself forget that she might someday have to leave. And now someday was here.

"We should get going," Devaney said.

Still off balance, Laura nodded slowly.

He frowned. "I'd rather you ride with me, but we can't leave your car here."

"Because it would look as if something bad happened to me."

He nodded.

"I'll have to call my boss," she said faintly. "If it's okay, I'll tell her it's a family emergency and make sure she knows I won't be back."

She glanced at Floyd. "So, we'll drive to Oklahoma City?"

"No," the older man said. "I won't be going with you. I'll meet you there later. Devaney has brought Enigma's jet."

"Jet?"

"The pilot is on standby," her new protector put in. "We can leave your car covered and in the hangar where the plane is stored. I'll follow behind you. Do you know how to get to the airport?"

"I didn't even know Pueblo had one."

After a last look around, she grabbed her winter coat and followed the men outside. Floyd put a hand on her shoulder.

"I wouldn't have brought Devaney here if I hadn't checked him out forward and backward. The director personally vouched for him. If I thought for one minute this guy wasn't on the level or that he couldn't protect you, I would've sent him packing."

Aware of how careful the marshal had been with her up to this point, Laura knew that was true. Even so, she was nervous. Vin was alive and as long as he was, she was in danger.

Devaney waited for her to lock up, then gave

her directions to the airport. In the darkness, he was nearly invisible until he slid behind the wheel of a dark sedan. She said goodbye to Floyd, then settled into her red compact. After the taillights of the older man's SUV disappeared, Devaney waved her out of the parking lot and followed.

He appeared able to protect her. She hoped he was, but what if she needed to be protected from *him*? The thought drew her up short. Where had that come from?

She drove through the quiet streetlamp-lit streets of Pueblo, glancing in her rearview mirror frequently.

The man who'd come for her stayed close as she battled a mix of resentment and fear and uncertainty.

Griffin Devaney had wrecked her manufactured life like an EF5 tornado. He hadn't just brought up her past. He was sweeping her right back into it.

Laura's aunt hadn't met them at the airport as expected. Instead, she'd had to rush Laura's father to the hospital.

Being back in Oklahoma City felt surreal. The plane ride and the composure of the man beside her had helped lessen some of the fear she'd felt at Griffin Devaney's appearance, but not the apprehension or the uncertainty. As a result, conversation had been sparse.

During the drive to OU Medical Center, she was jumpy. What if Vin somehow learned she had surfaced? What if despite his need, her father didn't want to see her?

She flattened a hand on her stomach, trying to still the flutters there. They weren't all due strictly to anxiety. Devaney set off surprising flutters of his own.

She slid a look at the solidly built man behind the steering wheel. Occasionally, light from the streetlamps slanted across him, the shadows doing nothing to soften the carved-rock line of his jaw.

What was his story? Beneath the nerves, the uncertainty and wariness, she was intrigued by the man who'd found her. More curious about him than she'd been about any man in a long time.

Uncomfortable with the realization, Laura forced herself to focus on the reason she was here, not the grimly handsome man beside her.

What had happened between her and her dad had been just as much his fault as Laura's, but she didn't know if Nolan Prentiss would see it that way. And it didn't matter. She had forgiven him and hoped he could do the same.

Not much had changed in the months since she'd been away from Oklahoma City. Though she didn't see anything new on the drive from the airpark, she was unexpectedly nostalgic at the sight of the illuminated dome of the state capitol as they traveled I-235 South.

Farther south and east than their destination was Bricktown, a bustling area of downtown that boasted restaurants, a ballpark and the arena for Oklahoma City's NBA team, the Thunder.

Everything might look mostly the same, but it didn't feel the same. Thirty minutes after leaving Sundance Airpark, she found herself at OU Medical Center. Griffin whipped his SUV into a parking spot in the lot of the hospital where her father had been admitted.

The temperature here was about the same as it had been in Pueblo and Laura snuggled her face into the collar of her heavy coat. Neither she nor her companion spoke as they rode the elevator to the seventh-floor oncology ward. Even though she didn't know Griffin, Laura was glad not to be alone. His quiet steadiness helped settle her somewhat.

They got off the elevator and turned left, passing an open family waiting area. Another bank of elevators sat at the opposite end of the long hallway. A second nurse's station served visitors in that area. Several yards away, Laura hesitated and Griffin stopped beside her.

"Are you nervous?" he asked.

"I— Yes." She hadn't faced her father in years. Though she intended to see him—she had come out of WitSec for this—she had no idea what kind of reception she would get.

The area was quiet, the only sounds the occasional beep of machines and the heave of a heater. After asking about Nolan Prentiss's location, she explained she was a family friend who had been asked to come. In answer, the pretty red-haired nurse at the desk gestured down the hall toward a patient room.

"Mr. Prentiss has already started his conditioning," the woman explained. "Before you go in, you'll need to put on this mask and gown."

"Conditioning?" Laura asked.

"He's undergoing chemo to kill his bad cells."

The tap-tap of a pair of heels interrupted them. Laura turned to see her aunt coming down the hall, shedding a mask and gown.

Looking smart in a pink sweater and dark slacks, the older woman rushed toward her and grabbed her in a big hug.

"Thanks for coming," Joy said thickly, her blue eyes bright with emotion. She lowered her voice. "I didn't know if I would ever see you again."

Laura had wondered, too. Tears burned her throat and she returned the embrace.

Joy stepped back. "You look beautiful. Your hair's grown."

She put an arm around Laura's shoulders. "You can see Nolan if you'd like, but he's heavily drugged and unresponsive."

"I won't go inside, but I would like to look in on him." She peeked inside the room, taking in the hospital bed flanked by an IV bag and a blood-pressure-and-heart monitor. Her gaze went to the man lying motionless under a light blanket.

Her breath caught. Nolan Prentiss, always trim and fit, looked emaciated. His normally ruddy coloring was gray, his blue eyes closed, his brow furrowed as if in pain. He didn't stir.

Laura sent a questioning glance to her aunt.

"He's on morphine for pain. He hasn't been conscious since we arrived earlier, but it's for the best."

"What pain?"

"In his back and stomach. His back started hurting about two weeks ago and his oncologist confirmed it was a relapse of the lymphoma. Nolan called me today when the pain became so severe he couldn't even stand up. I brought him straight here and they admitted him."

Laura swallowed hard, keeping her voice quiet. "Mr. Devaney said Dad was diagnosed nine months ago for non-Hodgkin's lymphoma."

"Yes, a type called diffuse large B-cell."

She had no idea what it was, but it sounded bad. Laura's stomach knotted. She couldn't remember ever seeing her father like this. She wanted him to open his eyes and look at her even though her emotions were a mix of love, regret and shame.

Torn between going in or leaving her father in peace, Laura shifted beside her aunt. Nolan's raven hair had turned completely white. He was frail. For the first time in her life, she thought of her father as something other than strong and unyielding. Life had taken its toll on him, just as it had on her.

"Let's come back later." Her aunt closed the door and steered her away.

Devaney fell into step on Joy's other side. The older woman gave him a quick hug. "Thank you for bringing Laura."

Griffin smiled, his hard features softening, his blue-green eyes warming.

The change in his face made Laura a little weak in the knees, which completely shocked her. She jerked her gaze away. Oh, please. She was tired. That was why she'd felt that little wobble.

Retracing their steps, they made their way to the waiting area they'd seen when they stepped off the elevator. Among the groupings of chairs, there was a television on the wall. One section of chairs was broken up with a small table and phone in the middle. A long couch sat on the adjacent wall.

People clustered in groups of two or three along the near wall. Laura walked across to the less populated side of the room with her aunt and took a chair. Griffin eased down onto the gray sofa.

Joy dabbed at her damp eyes, lowering her voice. "The person who originally volunteered to be Nolan's donor is ill. Thank goodness your blood sample was on file with the register. I was tested, too. Siblings have the best chance of having the same HLA molecules, but I wasn't a match at all."

"HLA molecules?"

"Antibodies that are proteins in the blood and could interfere with the success of the transplant. There's only a twenty-five percent chance that I would be a perfect match. The chances are even more slim that the parents or children of a patient will match."

Laura frowned. "But I'm a match?"

"Yes, praise the Lord." A determined look crossed Joy's face. "I've been praying that you would be able to help your father and now you are. God doesn't pay attention to percentages."

Still shaken by seeing her larger-than-life father in such a feeble state, Laura was hit with a sense of urgency. "What do I need to do? Shouldn't we get started?"

"You'll undergo some tests to make sure you're healthy enough to donate."

"What kind of tests?"

"Joy?" The red-haired nurse who had directed them earlier appeared in the doorway. Her name tag read Cheryl. "Sorry to interrupt, but I understand this is the visitor you want to be tested."

"Yes." Joy introduced Laura. "I told her she would need to be examined."

Cheryl smiled, her brown eyes warm. "It's just to make sure you have no issues. Even something that seems as inconsequential as a tooth infection can cause problems. Whenever you're ready, we can get started."

Laura recalled her father's fragile appearance. "I'm ready now. How soon will you know if I'm healthy enough?"

"Pretty quickly. The lab processes donor candidates ASAP in case we need to continue searching for a match."

Joy squeezed her hand and Laura met her aunt's sober blue gaze. "I hope this works."

"I have faith," Joy said.

Laura should, too.

The nurse walked out and Laura followed with Griffin right behind her. An hour later, she and her bodyguard returned to the waiting area to meet her aunt. Once Laura explained about the tests she'd undergone, Joy patted her hand.

"I imagine you're exhausted," the other

woman said. "We can visit on the way to my house. I fixed you a room."

"No," Griffin said. "She's coming home with me."

Laura jolted in surprise. "With you?"

"Yes. The one place I can guarantee your safety is my house."

Though Laura didn't like it, he had a point. She turned to her aunt. "He's right. I don't want to put you in danger."

"I don't want to put you at risk, either, but I wish we could spend some time together."

"So do I." Leaving her family behind had been much harder than Laura had anticipated. She had never realized how defined she was by whom she loved and who loved her, who was in her life. She glanced around the waiting area. "I could sleep here."

Devaney was shaking his head before she even finished. "Not a good idea. Joy, you can stay at my house, too. In fact, I'd feel better if you did."

"What if someone finds out?" Laura half whispered. "Won't that put her in danger?"

"You won't leave or arrive together."

He turned to Joy. "Boone or Sydney will get you to and from my house without being tailed. Laura will be with me."

"That sounds good." Joy hugged Laura briefly. "Boone and Sydney work at Enigma.

Staying with Griffin, we'll be able to catch up. I'll go home and get some things, then meet you at his house."

"All right."

The three of them walked toward the elevator. Griffin stayed close.

He'd said he would do his best not to let Vin find her and he hadn't been kidding. Devaney hadn't left her side since they'd flown out of Pueblo. As much as she hated to admit it, she found his presence reassuring. And now she was going to his home.

The elevator doors opened and the three of them stepped inside, moving toward the back. A husky boy who looked to be in his late teens slouched in one corner, hands in his jeans pockets, the hood of his red sweatshirt pulled over his eyes.

An athletic-looking man stood along the opposite wall between a young boy and young girl who each clasped one of his hands. Two older women filled that corner. Cheryl, the red-haired nurse who had taken Laura for her tests, moved to the back.

"Time for my break," she said upon seeing them. She turned to the side to accommodate a small slender man with a long gray ponytail dangling from under a grimy baseball cap.

As Griffin and Laura shifted to give the newcomers some room, she noticed he kept her between himself and Joy.

When the elevator reached the lobby and the doors opened, the passengers angled so the older women could exit first. The movement caused Laura to scoot closer to her bodyguard.

The remaining occupants surged forward, knocking her off balance for a second. Someone bumped her from behind and Laura reflexively reached for the wall. Instead, she got Griffin's iron-hard biceps. Just as she steadied herself, Laura felt a sharp prick in her free arm.

She jerked, drawing in a jagged breath at the shooting pain.

Griffin immediately pulled her closer, allowing the rest of the group to disembark. "What? What is it?"

"Something just stuck me." She started to pull up her sleeve, then stopped short at the sight of a syringe dangling from her sweater sleeve. She made a noise and Griffin's hand settled heavily on her shoulder as he turned her slightly toward him.

Though no one was waiting for the elevator at the moment, Griffin ushered her and her aunt off. After they entered the area that opened into the lobby, he stopped them and took Laura's arm, examining it carefully.

Joy leaned in. "What is that?"

"A syringe," Griffin said grimly.

Laura reached for it, but he grabbed her hand.

"Don't touch it." He glanced at Joy. "Do you have a tissue?"

"I have a handkerchief."

As her aunt pulled the cotton cloth from her purse, Laura remained still, her arm smarting. The hankie was one made by Joy, her first name embroidered with a signature flower in place of the *o* in her name. Laura had one just like it.

Using the handkerchief to pluck the needle out, Griffin studied the clear liquid in the syringe. "It's full of something."

"Drugs?" Laura's voice shook. Or something worse? she wondered.

"I'll find out. How's your arm?"

"It stings, but the pain is already starting to fade." She pushed up the fabric to reveal a short raw scratch just above her elbow.

Concern clouded Joy's eyes as she looked at Griffin. "Do you think someone did this on purpose?"

His face darkened. "I don't know."

Laura's gaze shifted to the man beside her, her heart suddenly pounding hard. "If it was deliberate, why stick me in the arm? That seems as if it would draw too much attention from others in the elevator."

"Maybe they meant to stick you somewhere else."

She swallowed hard.

"Like in the side or the hip." Devaney gently eased her closer to the wall. "All of the jostling as people left the car could've made them miss their target. I doubt they meant to leave this syringe behind, but it snagged in your sweater. They couldn't retrieve it without drawing attention to themselves."

Mouth dry, she stared up at Griffin. She mentally reviewed all of the faces of the people who'd ridden the elevator with them, but she couldn't remember anything unusual or suspicious or recall anyone being jumpy.

A muscle working in his jaw, Griffin's gaze scanned the milling crowd.

"Do you see anything?" she asked.

"No one running away or looking guilty or even appearing to be interested in us."

Dread curled through her as Griffin cautiously wrapped the needle in the handkerchief and slid it into his coat pocket. He then took Laura's elbow and steered her toward the hospital entrance.

Joy followed. "What are we going to do?"

"First I'm going to figure out if there's a security camera in the elevator," he said. "Then when we get to my house, Sydney can draw some of Laura's blood. She has medic training. We'll send that along with the syringe to a lab we use. Then we'll know the contents and if any of it is in your blood."

"Does it really matter what's in the syringe?" Laura tried to temper her tone, but fear gave her voice a sharp edge.

"Once we determine the contents," he said in a low voice, "we'll know if they meant to harm you."

"And how badly," Laura finished quietly at the realization.

Joy's gaze went from her niece to Griffin. "Do you mean it might have killed her?"

"Can't dismiss the possibility."

"Oh, dear." The older woman's face tightened with apprehension. "Could Vin have had anything to do with this?"

Griffin's steel-hard gaze slid to Laura's and held. "We have to assume so until we know differently."

Laura struggled to breathe past the crushing pressure in her chest.

Could her ex have already found her? If so, how?

TWO

An hour later, Griffin had Laura settled in his house. Back at the hospital, she'd lost all color and had outwardly trembled at the thought that Arrico might have already found her. Griffin hadn't seen fear like that since his last rescue two years ago. He didn't like seeing it on someone he was supposed to protect.

She'd hardly spoken during the drive out west of Oklahoma City. Joy was on her way, escorted by Sydney Tate, Enigma's sole female operator. To be safe, Griffin had disinfected Laura's arm. Then they had eaten dinner. She'd been quiet throughout the meal, a sense of dread palpable in the room.

Before they'd left the hospital, Griffin had checked the security footage from the elevator. So as not to alert anyone else in the hospital, he had managed to keep that between him and the guard in the equipment room. It was impossible to tell who had jabbed Laura with the syringe.

It could've been the kid in the hoodie or the nurse or the guy who'd gotten on last. The nurse would certainly have easy access to a syringe. Since they hadn't reported the incident, only they and the person with the syringe knew what had happened. Before Griffin gave out that information to the nurse, he would observe her, see how she behaved around Laura. Griffin stood in the doorway between his kitchen and living room. Fluorescent light brightened the room, gliding over the white cabinets and light blue walls. His guest sat at the kitchen table in front of the bay window.

It was weird having a woman here. He never had, not in this house, anyway. He didn't bring dates here. In fact, he hadn't *had* a date since his broken engagement to Emily. And so far in this job, he hadn't needed to host a client— male or female.

Papers were scattered across the table's oak surface and Laura's head was bent as she worked on the mountain of forms needed by the hospital and the transplant doctor. Her black hair was down now, sliding around her shoulders like a silky midnight cloud. He wondered if it was as soft as it looked.

She glanced up and saw him. Griff braced one shoulder against the doorframe. "How's your arm?"

"A little sore. Not bad."

"Getting through all of the paperwork?"

"There are a ton of questions, but I'm about finished." She furrowed her brow. "I almost signed my real name a couple of times."

"It's good you caught yourself."

"That's one of the reasons WitSec likes witnesses to keep their real first name and the same first letter of their surname."

"Makes sense." Griffin had never thought about it, but he imagined it would be second nature to sign or answer to your real name. "It probably helps keep any friends or relatives in the program from blurting out the wrong name."

She nodded, indicating the cell phone lying in front of her on the table. "Thanks for the phone. I called Floyd and explained that I'll likely be my dad's bone marrow donor."

Griffin walked over and picked up the burner phone he'd given her, planning to dispose of it downstairs in the computer room. "How often does Yates want you to check in?"

"Every day until the procedure is finished. He's planning to come down in a week or earlier if he needs to." When Griffin nodded, she continued, "I still can't believe I'm a match. From what Aunt Joy said, the doctor made it sound like it was a near miracle. I hope it makes a difference to my dad." She finally stopped writing and put down the pen, frowning. "I hope it cures him. I don't want to let him or Aunt Joy down."

"You won't. Just your being here helps."

Her gaze searched his and after a moment, she smiled. "It's nice to have someone to talk to about it."

It probably shouldn't be him. For a second, he was struck by the clear blue of her eyes. He didn't realize he was staring like an idiot until she looked away, pink blooming in her cheeks.

He gave himself a mental kick. What was he doing? He needed to focus on her protection, not *her*.

"Once Joy arrives, and we draw your blood, I'll send everything with Sydney to a lab we use," he told her again. He was nervous all of a sudden and couldn't think of anything else to say.

"How long will it be until we know something?"

"If there are no glitches, twenty-four hours or less. The lab will email the results to me."

"Is that safe?" Laura tucked a loose strand of hair behind her ear. "I know email accounts get hacked."

"Everything on these computers is encrypted."

"Good to know." She gave him a little smile, which hit him right in the gut. He didn't like it. Suddenly he felt as if the walls were closing in on him.

"There's not a lot here to keep you entertained. TV or a few books, mainly thrillers. Or my gun range."

"*Your* gun range?"

He nodded. "It's underground."

"Really?" Interest flashed in her eyes. "I don't know how to shoot, but I'd like to learn, especially after what happened in the elevator."

Being able to protect herself would give her some peace of mind. Griffin could do that. "If you're serious, I can give you some lessons."

"That would be great. I'd feel better if I at least knew how to handle a gun."

"Whenever you're ready."

She rose. "Now?"

He nodded. He wasn't wild about taking her downstairs to the security room, but on the off chance that she might be threatened here, he wanted her to know she had a secure place to go.

After straightening her papers, she followed him across the wood floor of his large living area, then through the kitchen before they moved into the laundry room.

Griffin opened the closet used to store the iron and ironing board, which also had a rod for hanging clothes.

He pushed a button on the bottom of the clothes rod and the back of the cabinet swung open, revealing a set of stairs.

"Oh, my word! Is there a secret room?"

Laura's question sparked a half smile. Instead of answering, he stepped inside and started down the stairs. Motion-triggered lights flashed on to show the way.

She followed. At the bottom of the steps, the space opened into a large room that housed all his computers and security equipment. His guest stopped beside him and Griffin punched in today's code, killing the laser security beams.

He started across the dark floor, then realized Laura wasn't behind him. He glanced back, stopping when he saw her stunned expression as she looked around the room with its long chrome table full of black monitors.

"This is like the Batcave!" she exclaimed.

That startled a laugh out of him. "Not exactly."

"Close enough."

He was still smiling when she moved to the bank of flat-screen monitors stretching in front of her. When was the last time he'd laughed while with a woman? He didn't know.

His chair was arranged so that he faced the door and the screens, allowing him to see the entrance at all times. Along the adjacent wall was a refrigerator/freezer and a black leather sleeper sofa.

"What is this place?" Laura studied the monitors that displayed all the rooms in the house and various places on the property. "You really are prepared for anything."

"If I need to, I can stay down here for a while."

"You mean like if you were under siege?" Her eyes twinkled as she gave a disbelieving laugh.

He didn't laugh, recalling the night that he and his team had been ambushed and under siege, resulting in the loss of his friends. He wasn't going to be in a vulnerable position again if he could help it.

"It comes in handy," he allowed.

"Impressive." Her gaze moved around the space. Past the restroom at the back and to the vault on the same wall.

"This is amazing," Laura murmured.

"If you get spooked and I'm not around, you can come down here."

"Are you planning to leave me here while you go to work?"

"You are my work, so no." He didn't miss the relief in her eyes. "This is a place you can come in case you need to. Plus there's another exit."

She scanned the room. "Where?"

"Through the vault." He led her to the large steel door with its engraving of the trident earned by all SEALs.

With an expression of awe, she stopped in front of the vault. "Wow."

She reached toward the engraving of the

eagle, anchor and flintlock that marked a sailor as a fully qualified navy SEAL. Griffin grabbed her hand. At the touch, a warm tingle spread up his arm.

Whoa, he thought, releasing her. "You aren't in my system and you'll set off the alarm if you touch the door."

"Oh."

"Let me show you." Stepping up to a recessed dark glass panel in the wall beside the vault, he bent so his retina could be scanned. After the approving beep, he placed his hand on the panel. It beeped again; then the vault lock clicked open.

"Unbelievable," Laura breathed. "This is just like in the movies."

"When we finish shooting practice, I'll put you in the system. I can delete your prints after you're gone."

"All right."

He opened the door wide and waited for her to precede him into the custom-made room.

She walked through the door, trailing a scent of spring freshness. "How long have you worked at Enigma?"

"Three and a half years."

"What did you do before that?"

"I was in the Teams."

"The Teams?" Her forehead wrinkled. "Like… sports?"

He almost smiled. "No, ma'am. The navy."

After a second, her eyes widened. "You mean you were a SEAL?"

He tensed, wondering how she would react. Some women treated them like superheroes, some like killing machines in a video game. They were just men. Men who'd learned the hard way to do hard things. "Yes, I was."

She didn't ask if he'd killed anyone. Instead, her question was "Are your teammates still SEALs?"

"No." He didn't talk about them. Ever.

She must have realized he didn't intend to say more. After a moment, she said, "Thank you."

His gaze shot to her. "For what?"

"Your service to our country."

There was no mistaking the sincerity or admiration in her eyes. Those were the last things she needed to feel for him. He didn't deserve it. Not after what he'd done. Not after his decision had resulted in the deaths of his friends.

"How did you meet my aunt?"

"She was a volunteer at the hospital where I had additional surgery on my leg."

"What happened to your leg?"

"Broken femur, gunshot, shrapnel." In the firefight that had killed his teammates. "Joy, uh, urged me to come work for Enigma."

Laura gave him a half smile. "I guess you

learned pretty quickly that she won't take no for an answer."

"I did." Joy's job offer had probably saved his life.

Griffin walked between the two walls that exhibited a number of guns, everything from an Uzi to a sniper rifle.

He gestured toward the waist-high center cabinet with its drawers of ammunition. "The ammo is in the third drawer down."

When she didn't respond, he looked over his shoulder. She stood in the doorway, mouth agape, blue eyes wide.

"How many guns do you have?"

"Seventy-five." In here. "This underground range is also an alternate way to get out, if you ever need one. I'll show you after we get to the practice area."

She joined him at the cabinet, picking up the box of cartridges he pushed toward her. "Your place is something else."

"I never could've built it if I weren't working at Enigma."

"What do you mean?"

"One of my first assignments was to rescue a man's daughter and he insisted on rewarding me."

"He must be the richest man in the world."

She wasn't far off, Griffin admitted. The man was a sultan. "He was grateful."

"I'll say." Her eyes sparkled. "Did he give you an island, too?"

"No." But he had tried to give his daughter to Griffin. He had barely gotten out of that without insulting the man. The woman had been stunningly beautiful, but she'd never had an effect on him. No woman had after Emily and that was the way he wanted it.

"Ready?"

Laura nodded, following him through the opening at the back of the vault. The long hallway veed into an area composed of three shooting stations.

She chuckled. "I feel like Jamie Bond."

He grinned. Despite the gravity of her situation and that of her father, she still had a sense of humor. He liked that.

She might look as though a strong wind would blow her over, but there was steel beneath that dainty shell. She'd testified against a vicious criminal. That took guts.

Before meeting her, Griffin had been curious. Now he was impressed.

In short order, he outfitted them both with safety goggles and ear protectors. The paper targets were already set up, so Griffin handed Laura a Walther PPK. The small gun would fit her hand better than some of his others.

After explaining how to engage the safety, he instructed her on loading the clip. As she slid the bullets in one by one, she glanced up. "How did you find me?"

"After Joy told me what happened, I touched base with an old friend."

"Floyd's boss?"

"Yes." He hadn't gone through the proper channels. He'd needed info and fast, needed to make sure he wasn't putting her in danger when he showed up. Bohannon, the US marshal he'd rescued two years ago in Eastern Europe, had been more than happy to supply Griffin with whatever information he needed.

It had taken less than an hour to get the name of the US marshal assigned to her case. Then Griffin had gone to the field office in Colorado Springs to speak with Floyd Yates and read Laura's trial transcripts and a copy of her file built by the marshals.

He demonstrated how she should stand and hold the weapon, then turned it over to her. She missed the target three times before finally hitting it. Using the markings on the paper, Laura hit center mass several times, although none in the same spot.

He urged her to try two shots to the chest area and one to the head. That gave her a little trouble, but she kept shooting, a fierce look of concentration on her face.

Joy had given him a picture, so Griffin had

known that her niece was pretty, but up close she was...more.

She was the kind of pretty that grew the longer you were with her. Direct blue eyes, thick straight black hair pulled back to show the fine line of her neck and jaw. A mouth that hinted at a ready smile despite the fact that her life had been ripped away from her.

He noticed a scar on her chin. Had she gotten that from Arrico?

She emptied her last clip into the chest area of the paper silhouette of a man's upper body. The sharp odor of gunpowder filled the air around them.

Griffin hit the button to mechanically bring the targets to them. After examining her shots, he smiled. "Not bad for your first try. Come down here and practice whenever you like."

"Do you mind giving me more instruction?"

"Not at all."

"Thanks." She studied her handiwork with pursed lips. "Hopefully, I won't need to defend myself."

Her words reminded Griffin that as long as she was out of WitSec, she was vulnerable. And his responsibility.

A beep on his cell phone alerted him to a text message from Sydney. "Your aunt should be here soon."

They walked up the hallway, their shoulders

brushing. They reached the vault door and Griffin moved out into the computer room. When she didn't immediately follow, he glanced over his shoulder. And froze.

She had stopped in front of the picture.

Taped to the wall was a photograph of him with his team. The four of them were on the beach at Coronado in board shorts, the sun setting behind them. They'd just returned from jump school and had gone to the beach to relax. He'd been so distracted by his protectee that he'd hadn't thought about the picture being there.

Her blue gaze met his. "These must be your teammates."

"Yes." He didn't try to temper the coldness in his voice.

"You all look like such close friends."

"Yes." He wanted to shut her down.

"I guess you can't talk about them. For security reasons?"

"Right." He *couldn't* talk about them, but that wasn't why.

She frowned, probably wondering why he couldn't seem to manage more than one-word answers. Now she would ask questions. Questions he didn't want asked and wouldn't answer. He hated the whole idea of it. It would remind him that they were all gone. Dead. Because of him.

The security buzzer sounded, signaling that someone was on the property. A quick glance at the closest monitor showed Sydney's gray SUV coming up the winding gravel drive toward the house. "Looks like Joy is here."

"Oh, good." Laura moved to stand in front of him, close enough that a strand of her hair caught on his gray T-shirt.

He saw curiosity and a brief flash of pity in her eyes, just long enough to make him stiffen. Then it was gone.

"I'm sorry." She gestured toward the picture. "For whatever happened."

She squeezed his forearm, then walked out. His chest hurt from her words. It was clear that she knew his friends were dead, but he saw no reason to confirm it. How could she know that? Maybe it wasn't hard to figure out, but it made him feel as if she were in his head.

The realization made him want to bolt. He didn't do personal, not after what had happened in Afghanistan. And not after what had happened once he'd returned home to Emily.

If Laura had been any other client, he would have passed her off to Boone or Sydney, but because of his friendship with Joy, he couldn't.

He glanced back at the photo of him, Ace, Davy and J.J. His jaw tensed.

Griffin didn't want to be responsible for Laura

Prentiss aka Parker, but he was. He wouldn't fail her the way he'd failed his teammates.

Last night at Griffin's had gone better than Laura had expected. She'd been comfortable and somewhat relaxed, but after what had happened at the hospital, she couldn't shake the fear that Vin had found her.

Though Griffin had stayed nearby, he hadn't crowded her. And for the first time since Laura and her father had their falling-out three years ago, she hadn't felt alone. Even with Vin, it had often seemed as if she were all by herself.

This morning she was still thinking about Griffin's reaction to her seeing the photo of him with his friends. The tortured look in his eyes had troubled her. It had been obvious something awful had happened. She didn't really blame him for not wanting to talk about it.

It wasn't her business. In another week, she would be gone and she would likely never see him again. Still, she'd wanted to know about the photo. And him.

Though she had tried not to dwell on his reaction, she wondered about it. Wondered about a lot of things. He knew a lot about her. She knew next to nothing about him. Except that she was finding it hard not to like him.

Sydney had arrived for Joy, assuring Laura they would meet her at the hospital. The brunette had an ease about her that made her easy to believe. Laura and Griffin had left soon after.

Now she and her bodyguard hurried across the hospital parking lot and into the warmth the building provided. As they stopped in front of the elevators, Laura removed her coat. The paperwork she'd brought added a little weight to her purse.

"So your new clothes fit okay?" Griffin asked in a deep rumble.

She glanced down at her dark purple sweater. "If it hadn't been for you, I'd be wearing the same clothes until my things arrived from Pueblo. I appreciate you stopping last night so I could buy what I needed."

"You're welcome." The barely there smile he flashed had her smiling back.

All in all, he had gone to a lot of trouble. "I'm sure you weren't expecting houseguests. Thank you for everything."

"Sure." He looked away, as if uncomfortable with the compliment.

No one else stepped into the elevator car and as Laura pushed the button for the seventh floor, so did Griffin. They quickly broke apart but just as it had earlier when he had entered her prints and information into his security system, the feel of his hand on hers lingered. Strong, warm, rock steady. She glanced up. "No word yet on what was in the syringe?"

He shook his head. "I expect to hear any-time now."

As the bell dinged their arrival, Laura looked up at the man beside her. "I hope my—Nolan's awake this time. After I turn in this paperwork, I want to see him."

As they exited, she lightly touched Griffin's arm. "I'd like to use the restroom before we check on him."

"Sure. I'll wait for you here."

She walked back past the elevators and down the sparsely populated hall, then pushed open the door to enter the ladies' room. Chrome faucets gleamed against the white countertops and sinks. The floor and stall doors were also white.

She finished quickly and moved to the sink, putting her purse on the floor at her feet. After washing and drying her hands, she bent to pick up her bag.

Suddenly something snaked around her throat and bit sharply into her skin. She registered a thin cord around her neck as she was jerked back against a hard masculine body. The cord tightened, cutting off her air.

Choking, she clawed frantically at his hands, trying to get her fingers beneath the razor-thin band. It tightened even more, pulling at her hair and crushing her windpipe.

Spots danced before her eyes. The edges of her vision went black and a surge of pure panic shot through her. She twisted, still trying to get her hands under the cord biting into her flesh. The man lifted her off her feet and she struggled, accidentally kicking the trash can.

Desperate for help, she kicked violently, connecting again with the can. She managed to slam the heavy metal container into the wall. Her vision blurred as she distantly heard what she thought was the sound of the falling can.

She felt herself fading. A scream welled up, but she couldn't get out even a sound. Terror flooded her.

Abruptly, the pressure around her throat eased and she fell, hitting her head on the corner of the sink. She was conscious enough to register a series of grunts and then a sickening thud against the tile.

Suddenly Griffin was on the floor beside her.

"Laura?" He leaned over her, moving her hair gently out of her face as he peered at her. "Laura?"

His face came into focus, his hard-edged features stamped with concern.

She lifted a shaky hand to her throbbing head.

"Can you breathe?" he asked.

She nodded, forcing words past her bruised throat as she gripped his hand. "What happened?"

"You were attacked."

It had come too close on the heels of yesterday's attack. Fear sliced through her like a blade, jamming her breath painfully in her chest. "He found me. Vin found me."

"Looks that way."

Everything went black.

THREE

It was the blood. There wasn't even that much of it, but the sight of it had images ricocheting through Griffin's mind. Seeing Laura crumpled on the floor brought back the ambush. The fire-fight. The searing pain in his broken femur as he carried Ace's body down the rocky terrain.

This wasn't the same. Griffin fought to push away the pictures. He carefully helped Laura to a sitting position, glad to see recognition creep across her chalk-white face.

Fear sharpened her pretty features. Eyes wide, she stared up at him. "Who just tried to kill me? Did you get them?"

Griffin shook his head. "I heard the noise in here and rushed to reach you. I only saw his shadow as he headed into the emergency stair-well. I headed straight for you, and Sydney went after the assailant. Did you see anything? Can you describe him?"

"No. He was behind me."

"Did you notice anything about him? Cologne? Distinctive voice? Scars or tattoos?"

Laura thought hard. "There was something on his left wrist or hand. It might've been a tattoo. I don't know. Everything happened so fast."

The tattoo possibility was something at least, Griffin thought grimly.

"Laura?" Joy rushed into the ladies' room, followed by Cheryl, the red-haired nurse. "What happened?"

"Are you all right?" The nurse moved closer, her gaze probing.

Laura struggled to stand and Griffin clasped her elbow to steady her. Once she was on her feet, he curled his hand lightly around her upper arm to make sure she stayed upright. She was still pale. And trembling.

Concern pinched Joy's features as she looked her niece over. "What happened?"

"It was nothing." Laura gave a wobbly smile. "I fainted and hit my head."

"Knocked over the trash can," Griffin added.

The last thing they needed was to draw attention to what had happened in here. That would bring hospital security at the least and maybe even OCPD. "She forgot to eat this morning."

Beside him he felt her surprise, but she recovered quickly.

"Yes. I became light-headed and passed out." Her story was good and would hopefully minimize the scrutiny. Griffin saw the objection on Joy's face and caught her gaze, hoping the older woman would understand to remain quiet. To his relief, she said nothing about the large morning meal they had all shared.

Cheryl's brow furrowed. "Your neck is chafed and you've got a bump on your head."

"I'll have a headache and a bruise." Laura touched the swelling at her hairline. "But I'm fine."

The nurse looked skeptical but followed Laura out the restroom door. Laura reassured the redhead once more before the other woman left them.

As Laura turned to Joy, the stairwell door opened and Sydney rushed through. She was flushed, her dark hair pulled back in a ponytail.

She reached them, green eyes sparking with irritation. "Lost him in the parking lot."

Joy speared all three of them with a stern look. "What really happened in there?"

Laura explained while Griffin stepped off to the side to speak with Sydney.

The brunette angled toward him, keeping him on her left in order to accommodate the hearing loss she'd sustained in a line-of-duty injury when she'd served as a sharpshooter on the SWAT team. Her gaze moved constantly over the area and its visitors.

"No sign of the assailant."

Griffin shoved a hand through his hair, frowning at the sight of the swelling on Laura's temple.

The man had slipped into the restroom, right past Griffin. What if he had arrived later? What if Laura had been hurt worse?

A greasy knot formed in his stomach. It wasn't the same as what had happened in Afghanistan and if he quit right now, it never would be.

Sydney elbowed him, eyeing him with a certainty that said she knew he was blaming himself. "This isn't your fault."

"I think Boone should take over," he said.

Joy and Laura walked up in time to hear him.

"Boone?" the older woman asked. She turned to Griffin. "Why do you think Boone should take over? Because that man managed to get to Laura in the ladies' room?"

He nodded.

Laura shook her head. "But you got to me quickly. I'm fine."

"See?" Sydney said quietly. "You're the only one blaming you."

Laura glanced from his coworker to him. "For what?"

Before Griffin could say anything, Sydney turned to Laura. "Would you like a different bodyguard? I'd be happy to step in. So would Boone."

"No, I don't want a new bodyguard. Why

would I? Unless…" She looked at Griffin. "Do you have another client or another job?"

"No."

She frowned. "Then do you have a problem with me?"

"No." Griffin dragged a hand down his face. "Not at all."

Sydney arched a brow as if to say "See?"

Laura stared up at him with confused blue eyes. "You probably aren't used to babysitting someone. Is that the problem?"

"It's not that."

"Then what?"

"Like your aunt said, that guy slipped right past me," he said through clenched teeth. "It shouldn't have happened."

"No, it shouldn't have."

Griffin mentally kicked himself.

"But," she continued, "it's not your fault that it did."

Sydney nodded. "That's right."

Laura gazed up at him earnestly. "I'd prefer it if you would stay with me through the entire process, but it's your decision."

There was no blame in her eyes or her voice. No resentment, either. It took a second for Griff to process that.

She probably wanted him to continue because she was too shaken by the attack to realize she'd be better off without him.

"I know you can keep me safe."

He wished he were half as sure as she sounded. "You do?"

"Yes."

"All right, then." He couldn't deny the warmth he felt at her vote of confidence. "Let's get back to my house."

She hesitated. "No."

"No?" Had she really just said that? Griff drew up short. "Why not?"

"I want to see my dad first."

"Not after what just happened," he said bluntly.

"This is the best time."

"How do you figure?" He tempered his voice, cognizant of the people around them. "Didn't you just say you wanted me to stay with you through this? That you thought I could keep you safe? The safest thing is to get out of here."

"I don't want to take a stupid risk and if you really think I am, I'll leave. But whoever tried to hurt me is gone. And probably won't try anything else today. Plus Sydney is here if you want or need any backup. I want to see my dad." Her voice cracked. "I *need* to see him."

Sydney had combed the hospital and grounds, looking for the assailant. There had been no sign of the guy. He was long gone.

"There might not be another chance," Laura said quietly.

She had a point. Griffin didn't like it, but Laura was right about this being the best time to see her father.

After the syringe incident last night and now this, it was plain that someone had tipped off Arrico to Laura's presence. If they stayed here, Griff could observe any suspicious behavior, see if anyone hovered around or seemed too interested in Laura or her father. Especially Nurse Cheryl, who had been nearby after both attacks.

"All right, I agree. Under one condition.

"What?"

"If I say it's time to go, then we go."

"Okay. Thank you."

He nodded. They were staying. And he was still Laura's bodyguard. He hoped she didn't regret her decision. He hoped he didn't, either.

After agreeing to meet Aunt Joy and Sydney later at Griffin's house, Laura and Griffin headed down the hall. Thank goodness he'd agreed to let her see her dad. Two attacks in the past two days told Laura she might not get another chance.

Griffin slid a look at her. "I'd really like to check out your neck and head."

"They're sore but I think fine."

"No nausea or dizziness from your fall?"

"No. Not yet, anyway." Laura hoped she

wouldn't suffer further ill effects. Time was short and her father didn't need any delays.

Griffin searched her face. "You'll let me know if anything changes? If your neck or your head gets worse?"

She nodded, stopping near the nurse's station to leave her purse and coat in a visitor's locker.

They reached her dad's room and she paused, surprised at the flutter in her stomach that had nothing to do with what had just happened in the ladies' room.

Griffin stopped, too. "Are you afraid he'll be worse off than you imagine?"

"What if he doesn't want to see me at all?" There, she'd said it. To a near stranger.

"I'm sure seeing you will make his day."

Laura hoped so, but after what she'd done, she wasn't so sure. Squaring her shoulders, she glanced up, surprised to see encouragement in his blue-green eyes.

She wanted to study his face. Instead, she turned toward the door to Nolan's hospital room, saying a quick prayer that things would go well. "This could take a while. He might not be awake and I'd like to wait until he is."

"I'll be here, no matter how long it takes."

"I appreciate that."

He nodded.

She donned the required paper mask and gown, then pushed open the door and stepped inside. She was glad to see the drapes were partially open and light spilled into the room. Stopping at the foot of the bed, she grazed the knot at her hairline. Hopefully, it wasn't noticeably swollen yet and her dad wouldn't ask about it.

Nolan lay unmoving as he had last night and now Laura noticed things she hadn't been close enough to see when she'd looked in on him. Dark circles beneath his eyes, the parchment-thin appearance of his skin. There were still a few threads of black hair sprinkled among the thick whiteness.

Overhead she heard the muffled thwump-thwump of a helicopter. The silence of the room was broken only by the hum of machines. Because she knew Griffin would allow no one to get past him, she addressed her father as she wanted. "Dad?"

He opened his eyes, fixing his filmy blue gaze on her for a moment before recognition flared. "Laura?"

His voice was tentative, as if he didn't believe she was real. "Yes, it's me," she choked out.

Her heart beat hard in her chest and she realized her palms were clammy.

"I can't believe you're here."

At his accusing tone, she stiffened, instantly defensive.

"Aunt Joy tracked me down. She told me you were ill."

"And you came."

"Yes." Was he glad? Angry? She could tell nothing from his flat brittle voice.

He blinked slowly, almost as if he was too groggy to stay awake. Laura moved up the side of the bed. If he told her to leave, she wouldn't do it. This might be her only chance—*their* only chance—to make any inroads. "I know this is probably the worst time to talk, but I really think we should."

"We should."

Relief flooded her.

Nolan peered hard at her. "What happened to your head?"

"Just bumped it. I'm fine."

After a long moment, he labored out, "How did Joy find you?"

"She had someone track me down."

"Someone from that agency of hers," her father guessed.

"Yes."

"Who?"

"Griffin Devaney."

"Good man." Nolan's eyes fluttered as if it cost too much energy to keep them open, but he did. "Did you come so you could be tested as a donor?"

"Yes, and I've been cleared to be your donor, but that isn't the only reason I came. I want to ask your forgiveness."

"No." He shifted on the bed, wincing.

Her heart sank, but she wasn't leaving until she'd said what she needed to. "At least hear me out."

"Not…what I meant." Slowly, he lifted a hand and made a feeble gesture for her to come closer.

She moved up beside him, catching a faint whiff of his Old Spice aftershave mixed with the zing of antiseptic. His usually smiling face was haggard and wan, fatigue marking his mouth and eyes. The realization of just how ill he was shook her once more.

He grasped her hand, his grip weak. "I'm the one…who should…ask forgiveness."

He seemed barely able to speak. Tears blurred her vision and she carefully squeezed his fingers.

"I never should've let you go," he rasped.

"*I* left *you*."

"Still, I should've kept trying to see you." His voice grew faint.

"Don't strain yourself. Let me do the talking, okay?"

"I…I have things to say, too."

She smiled. "I know, but I don't want you to overdo it."

"Okay."

"Even before I moved in with Vin, I knew how wrong things were between you and me.

Knew it was my fault." She found it encouraging that Nolan kept hold of her hand. "I've made so many mistakes."

"So have I," her father rasped.

After graduating from veterinarian school, she had stopped visiting him. He'd never approved of Vin and she'd needed a break from his constant criticism of her life. Still, Nolan had persisted in trying to see or talk to her. Things had been strained between them and the breaking point had come when she'd told him about her decision to move in with Vin.

Nolan had disowned her and she hadn't seen him again until the trial a little over a year later. He had come every day and attempted to speak to her, but she had refused. Another mistake caused by resentment and stubborn pride.

He moved as if trying to sit up.

"No, Dad." She pressed a hand to his shoulder, shocked to feel the sharp edges of his bones. "Stay still."

He eased back onto the pillow. "I should've tried harder to get through to you, shouldn't have let it go on as long as I did."

"That's on me. It wouldn't have mattered how hard you tried. I was too ashamed and embarrassed about all the stupid things I'd done. About how right you were about Vin. I couldn't face you."

"I'm not proud of the way I behaved, either."

He drew in a deep breath, pain creasing his waxy features.

Growing concerned, she eased closer. "Is there something I can do to help you with the pain? More morphine?"

"No. If I take more, it will knock me out and I want to talk to you."

She wanted the same. Who knew how many more chances they would have.

"I want to put things right between us," he said. "But I know it won't be easy. Can you forgive me for being so stubborn?"

This was more than she had hoped.

"Yes," she said in a shaky voice. "I need your forgiveness, too. I was a foolish, stupid girl."

"You're still *my* girl and you always will be. I love you."

"What I did was so wrong. You were right all along about everything." She wiped at her eyes, giving a small laugh. "I bet you never thought you'd hear that."

A ghost of a smile hovered on his lips. "I've missed you."

"I acted like an idiot."

"We both made mistakes, honey."

Laura could hardly fathom her strict unbending father admitting to mistakes. Perhaps the years had softened him. Or maybe it was the disease ravaging his body. She wasn't sure she deserved Nolan's understanding, but she wanted it. Wanted to start fresh for whatever time they had left.

The burden of guilt and resentment and shame she'd been carrying rolled right off of her. *Thank You, Lord. For his forgiveness and Yours.*

He was fading fast. Laura bent over him. "It's okay to sleep, Dad. I'll be in town until the transplant is finished. We'll be able to talk again."

If Vin didn't get to her first.

"My first filgrastim injection is tomorrow. I'll stop by and see you again if I can." She would have injections on five consecutive days. The drug would move more blood-forming cells from her bone marrow to her bloodstream in preparation for the donation. "Four days after that, I can make my donation and you can receive the transplant."

Nolan was fighting drowsiness and he looked even more pallid than when she'd come in. "Laura, girl, I…"

The door opened and Laura turned to see a frowning Griffin enter with a stocky bald man. Both were wearing paper gowns and masks. A clerical collar showed beneath the other man's protective garment.

Griffin's gaze went over the visitor's head to find Laura. "The pastor says Nolan is expecting him."

The other man came toward her, hand extended. "I've already met your young man. I'm Rick Hughes, a chaplain on staff here."

Laura doubted Griffin cared for the assumption that they were a couple, but like him, she wouldn't correct the error. Warily polite, she shook the man's hand. "I'm Laura Parker."

"Rick, Laura's my—" Nolan broke off, squeezing his eyes shut for a moment.

Laura held her breath and Griffin moved to stand beside her. She drew in his unique scent. He had instructed her and Joy to be careful about saying anything that might hint at the fact that they were related. Her dad knew this, too, but the medication lowered his guard. She hoped he didn't blurt something out.

Nolan struggled to speak. "Laura's my... donor."

Relieved, she glanced at Griffin, who looked relieved, as well.

"That's very generous of you." The pastor walked to the opposite side of the bed. "I've been praying with Nolan's sister, Joy. Maybe you'll be the miracle he needs."

"I hope so." She relaxed slightly, but her bodyguard didn't.

Instead, he eased closer, close enough that his arm brushed her shoulder, reassuring her.

After some quiet words to Nolan, Hughes

glanced at Laura. "When do you start your injections?"

"Tomorrow," Nolan answered for her. "She's not wasting any time."

Beside her she felt Griffin tense. "You seem to know a lot about the procedure."

"One of my parishioners had it done about three years ago."

"Do you make regular visits to this floor?" he asked the chaplain.

"If there are patients who request it, yes." Hughes smiled. "Sometimes a doctor will ask me to drop in on someone. After that it's up to the patient if they continue to see me."

"So you see patients in other hospitals?" Griffin asked.

"Wherever I'm needed."

"Have you been coming to OU Medical Center long?"

"Almost ten years."

"And before that?"

"I was a missionary in Honduras."

Laura frowned. It sounded as if Griffin was interrogating the man, although the pastor didn't seem to mind. Was her protector bothered by something or was he just getting information?

Rick's hazel eyes shone warmly at Laura. "How long have you known Nolan?"

Was the pastor making friendly conversation or fishing for information? Griffin must have wondered the same, because he shifted, putting his body slightly, protectively in front of her. "Several years," she answered.

"Yes," her father said weakly, still grasping her hand. "We've known each other a long time."

Hughes nodded. "I met Nolan during his initial hospital stay after he was first diagnosed."

"That was about nine months ago, wasn't it?" Griffin asked.

"Yes." Rick glanced at the patient, concern crossing his round features.

Laura checked her father. His eyes fluttered as he fought the effects of the painkiller.

She squeezed his hand. "We'll let you rest now."

She wasn't sure he heard her, but he gave her fingers a light squeeze. When his hold went limp, she gently laid his hand on his chest and studied him for a moment.

Griffin cleared his throat and she realized he held the door open, waiting for her. She quietly walked outside followed by the chaplain and Griffin, who closed the door.

Rick Hughes walked a few yards with them, then stopped in front of another patient room. "I need to drop in on someone else. It was nice to meet you both. I'll probably see you again if you visit Nolan."

Griffin said nothing while Laura gave a non-committal response.

"Please let me know if there's anything I can do," Rick offered.

He seemed sincere. "Thank you," Laura said.

As she continued down the long hallway with Griffin, she noticed that he frequently glanced over his shoulder. They stopped to pick up her things, then made their way to the empty waiting area.

"Are you suspicious of the pastor?" she asked.

"Right now I'm suspicious of everyone."

That was probably good, though the act of always being wary made her tired. She didn't want to leave her father, but she didn't want to take any chances, either. "Thanks again for letting me see him."

He took her elbow to steer her toward the elevator and inside. Despite his relaxed appearance, energy pulsed from him. She had no doubt he could move in one flat second if necessary. Before the doors closed, his sharp gaze scanned the hall like a laser.

Seemingly satisfied that she was as secure as possible, Griffin turned to her. "How was Nolan before I came in with the chaplain?"

"Frail, but he was alert. We spoke for a few minutes."

Hit all over again with just how fragile her father's health was, her throat tightened.

Griffin frowned. "Your conversation didn't go well?"

"It did." She sniffed, looking into his steady sea-green eyes. "He said he was glad I came. He forgave me."

"And you forgave him?" the former SEAL asked gruffly.

"Yes." They really had made progress. Relief and astonishment and gratitude flooded her. She dabbed at the sudden tears in her eyes.

Griffin looked confused. "Isn't that a good thing?"

"It's very good." She opened her purse, looking for a tissue. "Sorry."

"Here." A handkerchief with her aunt's trademark embroidery appeared under her nose, small and delicate in his large sun-darkened hand.

She glanced up.

He smiled. "Your aunt has given one to all of us at Enigma."

With a small laugh, she wiped her eyes. He flashed a half smile and her nerves shimmered in reaction.

Their gazes locked and something flickered in his eyes before they shuttered against her.

He glanced away. "Were you able to tell Nolan everything you wanted?"

"Yes," she answered slowly. "I wish we'd had

more time to talk, but the morphine makes him so groggy."

"Did *he* apologize?"

"Yes."

"Good."

Crumpling the handkerchief in her hand, she tilted her head. "Why is that?"

He shrugged. "Maybe I don't know the whole story, but from what I do know, it sounded as though he should."

For some reason, his words warmed her. "Thanks."

He nodded, searching her face.

She couldn't seem to look away from him. His rugged appearance was in stark contrast to the kindness in his eyes. She couldn't deny that she found him appealing. Very appealing.

She frowned at the unexpected, unwelcome realization.

"I'm not sure you'll be able to see him again."

Why had he said that? Because her father wouldn't make it?

Or you *might not*, she reminded herself, gingerly touching the raw mark circling her throat.

"Coming here is too risky. This may have to be our last visit to the hospital."

Her heart sank. At least she and Dad had started to put things right.

"Sorry. I just don't know if it will be a good idea to stop and visit him when you go to the clinic for your injections. Enigma has a doctor on call. I'll talk to her and see if she can come to my house to give you the injections."

Enigma had its own doctor. Wow. From the information packet she had been given to read, Laura knew the middle three shots of filgrastim could be given anywhere, but she hadn't considered Griffin might want to do it at his house. Having the doctor come there would restrict Laura's movements even more.

Which meant she'd be spending a lot more time with the former SEAL.

"Looks like I'll be taking further advantage of your hospitality."

As manufactured as her life had been in WitSec, things had still seemed more simple before she met Griffin Devaney.

She liked him, but she wouldn't be here long enough for that to matter. Even if she were out of WitSec and able to stay, these days she listened only to her head. She was all about smart, rational decisions.

And smart was *not* a six-foot-plus ex-SEAL with blue-green eyes and a slow grin.

FOUR

Things had gone okay for the rest of their stay at the hospital. Still, Griffin didn't breathe easy until he and Laura were back at his house late that afternoon. The assailant had gotten past him. He was rattled and that angry red mark circling her neck didn't help.

He still wasn't sure if remaining as her bodyguard was the right call, but he'd agreed. He wouldn't go back on his word. And she wouldn't be attacked again, no matter what he had to do.

On the ride home, he had asked several random questions in an attempt to determine if she had suffered a concussion. She didn't appear to have one. Now she sat at his kitchen table, her features drawn and tired. The knot at her hairline was now swollen to the size of a quarter and starting to turn blue.

Joy was on her way here with Boone Winslow, who was standing in for Sydney this evening. Opening his first-aid kit, Griffin took out a tube of antibiotic ointment and uncapped it. He started to give the medicine to Laura, but she looked completely done in.

He squeezed some ointment onto a cotton swab and leaned down, gently tipping her head to the side. "I'll try not to hurt you."

"I'm not worried." She gave him a faint smile.

As lightly as possible, he dabbed the ointment on the vicious-looking abrasion around her neck.

"Okay?" he asked.

"Just fine. Thanks."

Her silky hair hung across one shoulder, sliding across the back of his hand as he worked. Satisfied that he'd done what he could for her injuries, he capped the ointment and tossed it into the first-aid kit. Then he gingerly checked the knot at her hairline.

When she winced, white-hot anger rushed through him. Griffin wanted to pound the guy who'd tried to kill her.

"Good thinking to kick over that trash can," he said, easing down into the chair adjacent to hers. "Have you remembered anything else about the guy who did this? Besides the possible tattoo on his wrist?"

"No. I'll let you know if I do."

The light in her eyes was gone and Griffin found himself wishing he knew how to put it back. "How are you feeling? Hungry?"

"Not really."

"Do you need some ibuprofen for your head or neck?"

"No, thanks." She didn't seem to need or want anything. Maybe her time in WitSec had taught her that. If Griffin hadn't thought she was strong before, he sure did now. Not only because she was still standing after being attacked twice in the past forty-eight hours, but also because she was still determined to do whatever was necessary to help her father.

Griffin couldn't comprehend how she seemed able to just forgive her father or how her father could've forgiven her so easily. He knew it *couldn't* be that easy. Could it? He'd never heard of anyone who'd done anything like that. He sure hadn't forgiven Emily and they had broken up almost four years ago.

He searched his mind for a way to keep Laura engaged. "How long has it been since you've spoken to your dad?"

He expected her to say ten months, the length of time she'd been in WitSec.

"My graduation from vet school, three years ago. We didn't part on good terms."

He shifted toward her. "What happened?"

"I rebelled. Against my dad and God. It started after my mom died from cancer. It was a pattern of bad behavior that went on too long."

"Until you turned evidence on Arrico?"

"Yes, although that didn't fix things with my dad."

"Were things always rocky between you two?"

"Not until my mom passed. I was seventeen, a junior in high school, and spent as little time as possible with him. The guys I dated were his complete opposite. Forbidden. I grew apart from him and apart from God, too."

"Maybe God grew apart from you," Griffin suggested quietly. That was what had happened to him on an Afghan mountain four years ago.

"I told myself that for a long time, but the truth is God was always there. I'm the one who turned away from Him."

Griffin wasn't sure he agreed. He'd lost God during a disastrous mission in the Hindu Kush that had also cost his career and the lives of his three teammates. God's absence had been confirmed when he'd returned home and Emily had dumped him for someone else. "You met Arrico when he brought his injured dog into the school's teaching vet clinic?"

"How do you know that?" she asked sharply.

"Marshal Yates and the trial transcripts."

After a moment, she continued, "Back then I was looking for trouble. Vin asked me out. I accepted. Two months later, I moved in with him. Bad decision in more ways than one."

Regret was written all over her pretty face. "Which you realized the night he hit you?"

Her eyes narrowed. "Before that, actually, but that's when I finally left."

"So, you found evidence of his drug dealing and human trafficking, and took it to the FBI?" he prompted.

She nodded. "The case didn't go to trial for a year and I was under FBI protection until it wrapped up."

"Then Arrico tried to kill you in a drive-by shooting. Which explains why you're in Wit-Sec."

"Did Floyd also tell you that?" she asked accusingly, her voice taut.

He realized she must feel that her life wasn't her own, which it wasn't. "The Marshals moved you to Pueblo and you've been there ten months, safe and sound."

"Until now," she muttered.

He tried to imagine how he would feel if his control were taken away like that. "You seem okay with giving up your life."

"Do I?" Her blue eyes were weary. "I wasn't at first. I was angry and bitter and resentful. WitSec was my *only* option or I wouldn't have done it. The cost is too high. You lose *everything*."

Griffin had never thought about it, probably like most people.

"I still have my moments. Then I realized I didn't want to live that way. I started to pray and read the Bible regularly. After that I began to feel some peace."

"You can be at peace even if you have to live as someone else for the rest of your life?"

"I think so. I intend to try."

"You came back knowing you'd probably have to disappear again."

"If my father dies, I would regret not having done everything I could to save him, regret not trying to patch things up. Things between us were bad before any of the stuff with Vin. If Dad dies, I would never get another chance. I don't want to stand before God and say that I didn't try to mend fences with him."

Griffin didn't understand why anyone would turn their back on family. He would never have done that. If he'd had a family, that is.

One of the reasons he'd become a SEAL was because he wanted to be a man worth something, wanted to belong somewhere. And he had, until he'd lost his brothers-in-arms.

They'd been his family. Now they were gone. He'd come home and gotten help for his PTSD, but that hadn't been good enough for Emily to give them another chance. Some bitterness still lingered. Was Laura able to put the past behind her because of her faith?

Griffin had learned that he could depend

only on himself and so far, so good. He might not understand Laura's actions, but he respected them. There weren't many people who would try to fix something that had been broken for so long.

Griffin's phone beeped and he looked down to see a text message from Boone. "Winslow's here with your aunt."

For a second, Laura looked confused. "Oh, I forgot Sydney had a prior commitment and Boone agreed to bring Joy."

With all that had happened today, it was no wonder Laura had blanked for a moment. The door leading from the garage opened and her aunt came in followed by a tall lanky man with coal-black hair.

Concern in her blue eyes, Joy's gaze went to her niece's neck. "How are you?"

"I'm fine." She gestured toward Griffin. "Dr. Devaney took care of me."

Winslow arched a brow at Griffin, then stepped around the older woman, extending his hand to Laura and introducing himself. "You're as pretty as your aunt."

At the compliment, Griffin gave his friend a flat look even though he had learned Winslow's charm was sincere. When on a job, Boone's charisma could also be dangerous, drawing someone in before they realized it might be a mistake.

After the brief pleasantries, the other man slid a look at Griffin. "Is there somewhere we can talk? I got the lab results back."

The icy sharpness in his friend's blue gaze told Griffin the news must be grim.

"Results from the syringe?" Laura asked.

"Yes," Winslow said. "And your blood test."

Griffin motioned around the small circle. "Go ahead. We all need to hear it."

"The good news is Laura's blood work came back clear of infection or foreign substances."

"And the bad news?" she asked.

"It was pentobarbital," Boone said in a flat voice. "A large dose. Enough to put out a horse."

At Laura's questioning look, he explained, "It's a narcotic."

"Heavy-duty narcotic," Griffin added grimly. Whoever had tried to inject Laura meant business. "It's used for surgery patients, sometimes for seizures or people with insomnia. An overdose can be fatal."

"So, this drug is available at the hospital," Laura said. "Readily available to personnel?"

"I don't know about readily," Griffin said. "But it's definitely accessible."

"So, anyone who works there could get their hands on it."

"Probably not just anyone," Joy put in hopefully.

"But," Boone added, "it wouldn't be that difficult to obtain."

Griffin nodded. "Before, I only asked Ghost for interior elevator footage. I'll have him also check the hospital security footage *outside* the elevator. Maybe he'll see someone going into the lab or supply room or even coming out with a syringe."

"Who's Ghost?" Laura frowned.

"A buddy who's a former SEAL," Griffin explained.

Boone added, "He's also a computer genius. His nickname is Ghost because he can get in and out of anywhere without anyone knowing."

"Oh."

Griffin turned to Laura. "He's already checking into the guy on the elevator who was wearing a hoodie."

"Is he checking out everyone on the elevator?" Joy asked.

"Yes."

"Including the nurse, Cheryl?" Laura asked. "She's been nearby both times I was attacked."

"And Pastor Hughes was conveniently around after the strangulation," Griffin said.

"No!" Joy burst out, shock widening her eyes. "It can't be him."

"I hope it isn't, but we have to look at everyone. Especially those in the hospital who are around Nolan."

"Well," Laura said slowly, "the pastor does spend a lot of time there."

After what she had been through, Griffin wasn't surprised she shared his cynical views on that.

"You shouldn't think so ill of people, Laura," her aunt scolded.

"She has to," Griffin defended. "We all do at this point."

Looking thoughtful, Laura said, "If Cheryl has access to the drug, so do other medical personnel."

"True," Griffin said. "But they haven't been nearby after each of your attacks."

"But Nurse Inhofe works on that floor," Joy put in. "Her being there doesn't prove she's involved."

"And since we can't tell who stabbed at Laura in the elevator, I'll have Ghost check on the nurse as well as the pastor. We do know neither of them were the ones who attacked you in the ladies' room."

"Well," Boone said somberly, "whoever jabbed you with that syringe meant to kill you."

If possible, Laura went even more pale, the blue of her eyes stark against her skin. For a moment, Griffin thought she might crumple, but she didn't.

She lightly touched the swollen knot at her hairline. "I think I'll rest for a while."

"So will I," Joy said.

As the two women walked away, Griffin kept his gaze on Laura.

"She's impressive," Boone said quietly.

Griffin slid his friend a look. "What do you mean? Her looks?"

"Her guts." The other man grinned. "But I'm glad to see you've noticed how pretty she is."

A man would have to be blind to miss that, but Griffin kept the thought to himself. "I have to take her back to the hospital tomorrow."

"Why would you do that?" Boone's gaze sliced to his, his tone saying he thought the idea was crazy.

So did Griffin. "It's not my preference. Nolan's transplant doctor finished going over Laura's paperwork and needs a final meeting with her and her dad. Because of his schedule, he can only do it there."

"I don't like that."

"Tell me about it." Griffin dragged a hand down his face. "This is the most unconventional job I've had in a long while, but I have to make it work. Which leads me to ask if you can go with us tomorrow. I plan on asking Sydney, too. I need both of you."

"Sure. Let me know what time and the plan."

"Will do."

Giving Griffin a slap on the back, the other man left. Griffin stared down at the first-aid kit on his table. He couldn't get the images of Laura's injured neck and head out of his thoughts. Or that syringe dangling from her sweater.

It brought back that unfamiliar burn of anger. He knew emotion like that—any emotion— could be dangerous. It bordered on becoming personally involved and Griffin wouldn't go there.

But he would do everything in his power to keep Laura from getting killed. To do that, he needed to keep his focus on the job, not on his growing admiration for his beautiful charge.

Enough to put out a horse.

With those words screaming through her head, it had taken Laura a while to fall asleep last night. A long prayer had helped. She was trying to turn things over to God, but that had been a lifelong struggle for her. Though she had gained some peace, she was still afraid. But she also believed God had given her this chance to make amends with her dad. Because of that, she was determined to complete the blood donation process.

On their way now for her required meeting with her father's transplant doctor, she hoped there were no problems today. The rainstorm that had accompanied their trip to the hospital had put them both on edge. And things were tense enough with Griffin because of his reticence to bring her back, but neither of them had tried to change the doctor's mind.

If they'd made an issue of meeting Dr. Farmer at the hospital, it would've looked suspicious to him and the staff. Laura and Griffin agreed that the less attention drawn to them, the better.

But she knew Griffin had ultimately consented to return only because he had been able to snag both Boone and Sydney for backup. Her every movement had to be carefully planned and orchestrated. It was frustrating and tiresome.

Laura hated that she had to be in WitSec. Yes, it was the only thing that had saved her life, but turning in evidence and testifying against Vin had also cost her everything—her family, her identity. She knew it had been the right thing to do, but she felt the price every day.

She was glad that at least she would be able to visit with her father for what would probably be the last time. There was no way Griffin would bring her back again and she understood why.

At the hospital, Griffin let her out at the east entrance with Boone and Sydney. Just the short time it took her to get from the vehicle to the hospital's door chilled her to the bone. She could almost feel Vin's hatred of her, the vicious resoluteness to end her life.

Griffin's SUV almost disappeared into the

deluge as he drove toward the parking garage. His two coworkers stayed close in the lobby of the reception area with Laura but didn't hover over her.

A few minutes later, Griffin came through the doors, cheeks reddened from the chill, his eyes jewel-bright in the burnished copper of his face. He tugged off his black gloves and stuffed them into the pockets of his dark leather jacket. He made no eye contact with either Boone or Sydney, just cupped Laura's elbow and guided her to the elevator.

The pair of operatives casually followed.

Her father had been moved into the bone marrow transplant unit to begin conditioning. Which was a medical way of saying he was being zapped with chemo to kill his bone marrow and cancerous cells to make room for new bone marrow.

When the elevator reached the floor, Boone and Sydney stepped off first and discreetly looked around before motioning Laura and Griffin out of the car.

She and her bodyguard moved into her dad's room in the BMT unit. As was policy, both of them wore gowns and masks to protect the patient from any germs. They were also required to use hand sanitizer each time they visited. Today the curtains had been drawn to let in the light, which was a watery gray due to the weather. Laura could almost feel the frigid November temperature.

She had just managed to wake her father when the door swung open and a distinguished-looking man of average height with thick gray hair stepped inside.

"Hi, Dr. Farmer," Laura greeted the transplant doctor she'd met after turning in her mound of paperwork.

Randall Farmer's dark eyes warmed as he said hello to Laura and Griffin, his voice muffled behind his mask. "Nice to see you two again."

The physician asked her father a few questions, then went over the process for the next five days. "Your injections of filgrastim need to be done at a specific medical clinic. The nurse will give you the information before you leave."

"Why a specific clinic?" Griffin asked.

"Insurance." Dr. Farmer shook his head. "These shots cost thousands of dollars. If they aren't given at a place that's been preapproved by the insurance company, they won't pay the charges."

"Guess we won't be able to use Enigma's doctor," Griffin muttered.

"Guess not," Laura said.

The doctor tucked her father's chart under his arm. "Laura, do you understand that you aren't specifically donating bone marrow but peripheral blood stem cells?"

"Yes."

Griffin rubbed the back of his neck. "What's the difference, Doc?"

"Donating bone marrow is a surgical procedure, done under anesthetic and in a hospital. PBSC donation is nonsurgical and can be done in a donor center or clinic. Using a process called apheresis, Laura's blood will be removed through a needle in one arm and pass through a machine that separates out the blood-forming cells. The remaining blood is returned to her through the other arm."

"That's quite a procedure." Griffin looked a little shell-shocked.

Laura knew the feeling. Since she'd arrived, she'd had a crash course in terminology, timing and procedure.

The doctor turned to her. "I appreciate you meeting me here. Is there anything you're concerned about? Anything you'd like to ask?"

"Do you think Nolan will be ready for the transplant when I donate my stem cells in a few days?"

"If not the same day as your donation, then he'll be ready the next."

"All right." Laura was glad, but she was also sad. Once her stem cells had been collected, she would have to leave.

After checking her father's vital signs and making sure there were no more questions, the physician left.

She turned to her father. "We'll let you rest now. I'm headed to get my first injection."

"Wait," Nolan said weakly, his pale blue gaze settling on her. "Joy told me about the syringe in the elevator. What else has happened?"

"I'm fine. I don't want you to get upset or even think about anything except getting well."

"What else?" The older man's gaze went past her. "Griffin?"

Keeping his voice low, her bodyguard quickly related the incident in the ladies' room.

"So, Arrico definitely knows you're back." Nolan's eyes fluttered shut.

"Yes." Even though he'd insisted, sharing this with her father bothered her. "But I'm safe and I know I'll stay that way. I'd tell you not to worry, but it wouldn't do any good."

"Has there been any news of Arrico's movements?" Nolan asked.

Griffin stepped closer. "Boone has been monitoring him in prison. So far his only visitor has been his attorney. He's seen Arrico twice in the last three days."

"Do you think he's trying to find a way to angle for a new trial?"

"I don't know. Whatever I find out, I'll pass along." Griffin shifted, his arm brushing Laura's.

Nolan took a deep breath, causing her to wince at the pain on his face. "Do you think Vin's lawyer was involved in these attacks on my daughter?"

She knew the older man was worried, but he didn't need the added stress. "Dad—"

"Mr. Prentiss," Griffin said quietly, "we're watching the lawyer to determine that."

Nolan nodded weakly.

With a look, Laura urged Griffin toward the door. Before he moved, he turned back to her father. "Sir, I'll keep you informed. You can count on it."

"Thank you."

At the thinness of his voice, Laura leaned over and kissed her father's cheek. Her throat tightened. "This may be the last time I see you, Dad. I'll keep tabs on your recovery through Aunt Joy somehow."

The marshal would actually make the contact and pass on the information, but Nolan knew that.

"I love you, Laura. And again, I'm sorry."

"So am I." She struggled to hold back tears. She'd finally been able to reunite with him and now she would have to leave again. "I love you, too. Please rest so you can beat this thing."

He gave her a weak smile.

She squeezed his hand and felt him grip hers in return before she walked out with Griffin.

Boone and Sydney fell in line behind them as they moved down the hall. Laura blinked at the brighter light, swept with a mix of anger and compassion and a deep sadness.

"I hate seeing him like that," she said thickly, wiping at a stray tear. "He's in so much pain."

"I'm sorry," Griffin said gruffly. "I know it's bad, but he'll get through it."

"It's so hard. For him and for Joy. I wish I could take some of the pressure of caring for him off her."

As they walked, she lowered her voice so that only he could hear. "Once I finish my injections, I'll have to leave and Joy will again be doing everything. I'll only hear about Dad's transplant and progress through Floyd. I really hate that part of Wit—the program."

"I can see why. I don't know if I could do what you've done."

"You're a SEAL. You could if you had to."

"Maybe," he said softly.

Something in his voice sent her pulse cartwheeling. She glanced over, surprised to see admiration in his eyes.

As they approached the elevator bank, someone called her name. "Miss Parker?"

Glancing over her shoulder, she saw Pastor Hughes waving to her. He finished his conversation with a petite brunette nurse, then strode toward her and Griffin. Laura couldn't help but wonder if he was involved with Vin.

Sydney and Boone melted into the corridor, one easing toward an alcove and the other to the elevators. Laura knew they could still see her and would be ready for action if something happened.

She and Griffin retraced their steps, greeting the stocky bald man, who was dressed in a black sweater and slacks.

With a compassionate smile, he took her hand between both of his. "Have you started your injections?"

"Today's the first one."

"Ah. Will you be going to a donor center or medical clinic?"

Why did he want to know? Even if she hadn't caught Griffin's warning look, Laura wouldn't have answered the question. "I'm not sure yet."

"You were probably told that headaches or bone or muscle aches are side effects of the drug. I'll say a prayer that yours aren't bad."

"Thank you."

After another few minutes of small talk, the pastor bid them goodbye. Eyes narrowed, Griffin watched the man return in the direction he'd come from.

Laura glanced at her bodyguard. "What is it?"

"We only met him after the attempt against

you in the restroom, but he might've been aware of *you* before that."

It made Laura nauseous to think a man of God might aid someone like Vin, but Griffin was right. They just didn't know.

Boone and Sydney joined them in the elevator. Griffin explained how he and Laura knew the pastor.

"He's too curious." He glanced at her. "Why should he care where you get the first injection?"

"Right."

Once downstairs, Griffin told her to wait while he went to get the SUV. Neither of them wanted to risk her getting a cold or any other kind of illness. Boone and Sydney stayed near Laura. Weak light seeped into the spacious lobby as rain pelted the windows and glass doors.

Griffin headed toward the entrance, punching in a number on his cell phone.

"Ghost, I need a little more information." His voice faded as he moved away.

"Does Ghost have a real name?" Laura asked, half to herself.

"It's Alex Morales," Sydney supplied in a clipped tone.

Laura glanced up to see the woman's jaw lock and her green eyes narrow. "He's good at finding anything on anybody. Anytime he wants."

Sydney was clearly not a fan. Had Alex Morales uncovered something about the woman to put that tight look on her face? As Griffin disappeared around the corner of the building, Laura really hoped whatever Alex aka Ghost found would help keep her alive.

Griffin shouldered his way out the hospital door and strode to the end of the portico, looking both ways before he crossed the side street. The rain had let up, though the cold still cut right through him.

Several yards down, he noticed the pastor also walking toward the parking garage. Griffin frowned. The man sure had made it downstairs quickly.

"Devaney?"

Ghost's voice crackled over the phone. Frigid wind scratched at Griffin's face, cold raindrops peppering his neck and head. He flipped up the collar of his bomber jacket and ducked his chin into his coat as he entered the garage east of the hospital.

"Devaney?" Ghost barked, snapping Griffin back to the phone call. "What's up?"

"Sorry." He pulled his attention back to the reason he'd called. "Are you having any luck with that security footage?"

"Hoodie guy from the elevator visited someone in the oncology ward. I'm trying to find out who. As for the nurse, she's on plenty of footage, but I haven't seen her with a syringe."

"Could've been in her pocket."

"True."

"All of this is great info. Could you help me with something else?"

"Shoot."

Griffin wiped the wetness off his face as he walked into the shelter of the parking garage, his gaze searching for his truck. "Is there some way you could get me a photo or video of Arrico's lawyer? I know he's visited the prison twice in the last three days."

"Sure."

"Thanks." Griffin wanted to get a look at the attorney to see if his build or height resembled the man who had attacked Laura in the ladies' room. "I also need some information on a Pastor Rick Hughes. He's a chaplain here at OU Med Center."

Finding his truck at the top of the row, Griffin glanced around for the reverend but didn't see him. Behind him a motorcycle gunned its engine. Reaching the back end of his SUV, he hit the remote. The brake lights flashed and a beep sounded before the door locks clicked open.

"I'll call you as soon as I find anything," his friend said.

"Appreciate it." He disconnected and slipped his cell phone into his jeans pocket.

One of the reasons Griff liked Morales so much was, having been a SEAL, he operated on a need-to-know basis, just like Griffin.

The übertalented computer guru never asked questions unless it was essential in order to dig up more information for whatever Griffin, Boone or Sydney needed. Something had happened in the past between Morales and Sydney, but Griffin had no idea what it was. Neither did Boone. They just knew Enigma's lone female operative and their computer genius couldn't or wouldn't be in a room together.

The motorcycle drew closer, the noise ricocheting off the concrete walls and floors.

Griffin halted at the driver's side and grasped the door handle. Something hot whistled past his ear and he instinctively ducked. Before he could turn around, he felt another slight burn close to his scalp. Adrenaline blasted through his system as a motorcycle roared by in a blur. Griffin's thoughts caught up with his reflexes. Someone was shooting at him!

FIVE

Griffin dove for cover in front of his SUV, hitting the ground hard. His hand automatically went to the Sig Sauer tucked in his back waistband. He leaped up and raced down the side of his truck to the empty space next to his vehicle. He squeezed off two shots, running toward the bike. Suddenly the bike spun and nearly landed on its side. The driver corrected himself with a screeching stop. Tires squealing once more, the man sped straight for Griffin.

Thunder boomed and a loud crack of lightning echoed through the garage.

Griffin fired again, then threw himself to the ground, barely managing to escape the bullet that zipped past him. The bike rider swerved closer to the opposite wall, enabling him to better see under the vehicles scattered out on this parking level. He zeroed in on Griffin, only partially hidden under his truck.

He slowed and fired once more, the shell

shaving way too close for Griffin's liking. He leveled his gun to hit the shooter dead center in the chest, but the guy ducked, sliding his cycle low to the ground as Griffin pulled the trigger.

The shot hit the cement wall and bounced off. With his gun, he followed the punk's progress, firing again. The rider zigzagged down the aisle. Griffin's next three shots hit high on a support pillar. Thank goodness there weren't many cars in the parking garage today.

The man spun his cycle around, gunned his engine and again headed right for Griffin. He bore down, firing twice. Griffin took cover behind his truck, trying to get a look at the driver. The man's face shield was black just like his motorcycle helmet. He couldn't make out the guy's features.

The shooter sped out of the garage. Getting to his feet, Griffin got only a partial license plate number. The bike roared away, the harsh engine sound echoing off the concrete walls. The storm's rumble rippled through the structure, the noise reverberating sharply.

Dragging in the smell of oil-soaked cement and car exhaust, Griffin stood and moved to the driver's-side door, searching the area for the motorcycle or any bystanders. The roar of the motorcycle faded. The shifting shadows revealed no one, including the pastor. Hughes had disappeared, which again raised Griffin's curiosity.

The deluge of rain continued, water pounding against the building. Frigid wind tunneled through the garage, stinging his skin as he turned to inspect his vehicle. Two long creases marked the driver's side, ruining his black custom paint job. He found one bullet lodged behind the driver's-side door. Already wearing gloves, he dug it out and put it in his pocket. There were likely no prints on the bullet, but he took it just in case.

A second bullet lay under the truck and Griffin scooped it up, too. Shooting accurately on the run or from a moving vehicle was extremely difficult. That was the only reason Griffin's truck hadn't been more damaged from the shoot-out. Same for the several automobiles scattered throughout the garage. A level above him, a car started, the noise almost masked by the storm. He again scanned the garage for people. Still no one.

Griffin had kept track of the bullets in his clip and the number of gunshots from the shooter. He'd taken eight shots and the bike rider had fired six. He checked the area for the rest of the bullets and added them to those already in his pocket. He wouldn't report the incident to hospital security or the police. The last thing he needed was a swarm of people asking questions.

Laura.

He spun and sprinted back to the hospital, drenched by the pelting rain. Racing into the lobby, he was relieved to see her standing where he'd left her with Boone and Sydney on either side. He slicked back his wet hair and wiped the wetness from his face.

Searching for the pastor, Griffin glanced around the lobby, pausing when he saw Cheryl Inhofe. The nurse was walking to the elevator with a fit trim man about six feet tall. Griffin couldn't see the stranger's face.

He turned his attention to Laura, who stared at him with big blue eyes. His gaze skimmed over her, taking in the dark curtain of hair that rippled like silk against the tan wool coat she wore. She looked fine, exactly as he'd left her. "You okay?"

"Yes."

"Everyone else?" He looked over at his coworkers.

Boone and Sydney nodded, both of them reaching for the weapons beneath their coats.

Laura's gaze switched from them to Griffin. "What's going on?"

Moving closer to her, he kept his voice low. "Someone just shot at me."

"What!"

"In the parking garage as I was getting into my truck."

Boone and Sydney closed the circle around Laura. "Did you see the shooter?" Boone asked.

Sydney stayed near Laura's side, her gaze panning the lobby.

"It was someone on a motorcycle, black face shield on his helmet and dressed all in black."

Dismay crossed Laura's face. "Like the pastor."

"Yeah." Griffin dragged a hand down his face. Could Hughes have been the shooter? If not, had he *seen* the shooter?

Laura shook her head, shock and confusion on her face. "Why would someone shoot at you?"

"So it would be easier to get to you," Griffin said grimly.

Fifteen minutes later, Griffin's words still chilled her. It had never occurred to Laura that he might become a target himself. Yes, she understood there was danger simply in the former SEAL being her bodyguard, but for Vin to come after him directly? It only emphasized her ex's determination to get to her. Her head spun.

Griffin carefully steered the SUV onto the wet streets that would begin icing before too long if the temperature dropped. In another vehicle, Boone and Sydney followed at a distance, keeping an eye out for someone dressed in all black on a motorcycle or anyone who might be tailing them.

They were headed to the insurance-approved clinic on the northwest side of town. Griffin was getting Laura away from the hospital and any further risk there. She was fine with that.

Between the attempt on her bodyguard's life and this being probably the last time she would see her dad, Laura could barely process everything. What would happen to her or her father if Griffin was injured? Or worse?

Just then he glanced over at her. "Are you sure you're okay?"

"Are *you*?" She searched his sun-burnished features, comforted by his clean masculine scent. "You seem so calm. Vin just tried to have you killed. You didn't sign up for that."

"It's part of the job sometimes."

She shook her head, her admiration for him growing even more. "I must be naive. I never thought Vin would come after you. I mean, I understand you're putting yourself between me and him, but—" Her voice cracked. "A drive-by. He tried to kill you the same way he tried to kill me."

"Hey, we're both still here."

He gave her a reassuring smile and she struggled to move past the shock of the ordeal, the way he had.

His gaze switching between the rear-and

side-view mirrors, he changed lanes. "When I went to the parking garage, I saw Hughes there, too."

Laura frowned. Why did Griffin think that was suspicious?

"He vanished right before that rider started shooting."

"And you think the shooter was the pastor?" she asked.

"Can't rule him out." Griffin hit a button on the navigation screen and a message flashed that his phone was now connected via Bluetooth. "I'm calling Ghost to see if he has any information yet on Hughes or the nurse."

Laura nodded, knowing she needed to stay silent so Griffin's friend wouldn't be aware of her.

The call went through and a deep masculine voice came through the stereo system.

The other man chuckled. "Miss me already, Devaney?"

"You know it."

Laura couldn't get over how calm Griffin sounded. Someone had just shot at him!

He turned the heater up another notch. "I wondered if you had anything yet on the names I gave you earlier."

"Some. We can start with what I've found so far and I'll keep looking as we talk."

"Sounds good." Griffin turned north onto the highway.

The sky grew darker. The windshield wipers made a steady swooshing sound as they cleared the water from the glass.

"Here we go," Ghost said. "Cheryl Inhofe, thirty years old, registered nurse. She used to work at the penitentiary in McAlester."

Laura's attention zeroed in on the speaker.

"She worked there three years," Griffin's friend said.

Which was plenty of time for the woman to have met Vin, Laura thought.

"She took the job at OU Medical Center about eight months ago."

Managing to hold back a sound of surprise, Laura's head jerked toward Griffin. The speculation in his eyes hinted that he thought the same thing she did. That was about a month after her father had been diagnosed and begun treatment the first time. Surely the timing wasn't a coincidence.

Excited that Griffin's friend had so quickly tied the nurse to Vin, Laura's heart sank when Ghost continued, "Got some stuff on the preacher, too."

She hoped it wasn't as incriminating as what they'd learned about the nurse.

"Richard Hughes, thirty-three, single, degree from a seminary in Nogales, Mexico. He's now an assistant minister at a community church in Oklahoma City. He also spent time at McAlester, but on the right side of the glass."

Disappointment hit her hard. It was hard to accept that a supposed man of God might be involved with her murdering ex.

Ghost's deep voice continued. "Hughes worked with the penitentiary's Religious and Volunteer Services for a couple of years, started a prison ministry there."

"Was he the prison's chaplain?" Griffin checked his side mirror before changing lanes.

"No, just a volunteer. He answered to the volunteer agency chaplain. About six months ago, he moved to Oklahoma City."

And now worked at the same hospital where Laura's father was a patient. At the same hospital where a former coworker, known to him or not, now worked. Another coincidence? Even Laura didn't believe that. Had Hughes and Cheryl Inhofe known each other in McAlester?

Griffin startled her when he asked that very question.

"There's no evidence of that yet," Ghost said. "But there is something else you should know. Both of Hughes's parents spent most of their lives in prison."

Stunned, Laura's gaze met Griffin's.

Morales continued. "He was raised by his grandmother. His mother was in and out of the joint for check and prescription fraud. His dad was a drug runner and killed someone during a deal gone bad."

That didn't mean the chaplain was like them in any way, Laura told herself. But she knew it could be difficult to get out of such a life.

"Thanks, man," Griffin said. "Let me know what else you find."

"You got it."

"Oh, one more thing. Can you find out if Hughes or the nurse has a motorcycle?"

"Will do."

Griffin disconnected the call, easing the vehicle over into the right lane.

"What do you think about the pastor?" she asked.

"There's a reason they say the apple doesn't fall far from the tree."

"Still, Rick Hughes could've chosen a completely different life than his parents."

The skepticism on her protector's face said that he didn't buy it. "The time Hughes spent at McAlester would've been plenty of time for him to meet Arrico or even form a relationship with him."

Laura's stomach knotted. "All Vin had to do was say he was interested in the Bible study provided by the prison ministry and he would've been able to participate."

"Right," Griffin said grimly.

She didn't want to believe the worst of Rick Hughes or Cheryl Inhofe, but until she and Griffin knew more, Laura had to assume that neither of them were who they appeared to be.

With all that had happened since her arrival, Laura felt as if she had been in Oklahoma City for three months, not three days. Now both she and Griffin had been targeted. She wanted to know more about this man who had nearly taken a bullet today. He seemed much more at ease about him being in the crosshairs rather than her.

Just as she and Griffin had finished supper, his friend Alex Morales had called with some information. Records showed that neither the pastor nor the nurse had a motorcycle registered in their names, but that didn't mean they couldn't get access to one.

Griffin wanted to ask both the pastor and the nurse some questions, but he couldn't risk confirming that Laura was alive in case one or both of them were involved with Arrico. Laura's ex might be getting information on her, but Griffin wasn't going to tip his hand about who he suspected of being in cahoots with the felon. The closer Griffin played things to his vest, the better the chance of drawing out those who were aiding the criminal.

He wanted to see who visited the reverend,

see how the man spent his off time. He planned to surveil Hughes tonight. Boone would stake out the nurse while Sydney accompanied Joy to a church function.

Griffin had told Laura she didn't have to come along, but he would feel more comfortable if she joined him. She felt the same despite the side effects she'd suffered from her first fil-grastim injection. Thank goodness the nausea and muscle soreness weren't severe.

She had to take comfort in the fact that she was helping Nolan. If things went as planned, her stem cells would save his life. Still, her heart was heavy. She'd thought someday, somehow, she might be able to leave WitSec and come home. Right now that didn't seem possible.

An hour after supper, Laura sat in the SUV with Griffin as they watched Pastor Hughes's house. Luckily, the rain had let up to an intermittent drizzle, so they could see clearly enough. The modest colonial with red brick and black shutters was located in a cul-de-sac of a well-established neighborhood.

Because they didn't want to be noticed, he couldn't leave the truck running. In an effort to keep her warm and prevent her from getting sick, Griffin had supplied blankets, as well as heat packs for her feet and coat pockets. He'd shown up with coffee for himself and hot cocoa for her. The thick blanket she'd wrapped around herself kept her warm and cozy. He, on the other hand, had tossed his coat and gloves into the backseat of the SUV, saying his jeans and flannel shirt kept him plenty warm.

Griffin's windows were too dark to see through and there were enough automobiles parked on the street that one more wouldn't be obvious.

Water ran along the curb and into the street. Hughes's porch light glowed in the chilly night like a frosty halo. Other front house lights burned in the darkness.

Griffin glanced at her. "Doin' okay over there?"

"Yes."

As it had been since their arrival, the pastor's garage door was closed. Earlier Griffin had slipped out of the SUV and up to the reverend's house to make sure that the man was indeed inside. So far there had been no activity.

A car crept past, heading out of the cul-de-sac as it splashed down the middle of the street. Griffin watched in the rearview mirror.

"Ghost sent me the prison's security footage of Arrico's lawyer." He passed his cell phone to her and pushed a button, bringing up a screen. "The guy has a similar build and height to the jerk who attacked you in the ladies' room."

Laura cupped a hand around the screen so only she could see the light from the video.

Tension stretched across her shoulders as she viewed the footage. "You're right. Do you think it could really be him?"

"I'll have a better idea after I observe him tomorrow."

She returned his phone. "Do you really think an attorney would try to kill me?"

"I don't know why not. Our other suspects are a preacher and a nurse."

"Good point."

"Besides, Ghost has gone through the security footage from the prison and Arrico's attorney wasn't at McAlester during the time of your attack. So far his whereabouts yesterday are unknown."

Comprehension drew her up short. "So he could very well be the one who tried to strangle me at the hospital."

Griffin nodded.

She blew out a shaky breath. "Vin really hates me for putting him in prison."

"Your turning him in and testifying may not be the only reason he's after you." Griffin rested his left wrist on the steering wheel.

"What do you mean?"

"When his father got pneumonia and died, Arrico wasn't allowed to say goodbye or attend the funeral. It's possible he blames you for being denied the chance to pay his last respects."

"I had no idea his father had died. It makes

sense he would blame me. He's vengeful. He showed that trait more than once. Can I pick 'em or what?" she muttered, then sipped her hot chocolate.

Thank goodness she'd finally realized what a mistake she'd made with her ex. A mistake she had paid for by losing all ties to her former life.

"You shouldn't beat yourself up." Griffin took another drink of coffee. "We've all misjudged someone."

"Even you?"

"Even me."

"I find that hard to believe." Glancing over, she found him staring out the windshield. She turned slightly toward him, drawing in his clean scent. "Was it someone you had to walk away from, the way I did?"

After a moment, he said, "She walked away from me."

"She?"

"My fiancée."

Laura started, her cocoa sloshing in the insulated cup. "You were engaged!"

"Don't sound so surprised," he said wryly.

"I'm not— Okay, I *am* surprised."

He shot her a look.

"What happened?

A sudden tension sprang up between them, but she couldn't let it go. Not yet.

"You don't have to answer, but you know

everything about me, especially concerning my horrid judgment in men. Seems like I should know *something* about you."

He pinched the bridge of his nose. "She found someone else while I was deployed, although she didn't tell me that until a month after I had returned."

Laura was surprised, both at his words and the fact that he'd answered. "How long had she been seeing that someone else? Since you were first called up?"

He shook his head. "Since right before I came home."

He'd been wounded when he had returned. What kind of woman left a man who was injured? A man who had so far shown himself to be steady and loyal. He was definitely loyal to Laura's aunt and his coworkers.

Laura doubted she would ever know the whole story, but the thought of someone doing him wrong irritated her. And she understood the kind of anger he must've felt, toward not only his ex but also God.

He'd been betrayed by someone he loved and so had Laura.

Without thinking, she reached over and laid a hand on his flannel-clad arm. It felt like rock beneath her fingers. "I'm sorry that happened."

Griffin's eyes widened at her touch, but he didn't pull away. Instead, his gaze met hers.

There was something in the blue-green depths. Interest. The realization had her heart thudding hard. She slowly pulled her hand away, shocked to admit that she was attracted to him. More so than she had been to any other man, including Vin.

Griffin cleared his throat and moved his attention to the window and the hazy night. Laura did the same on her side of the truck.

She'd been so wrong about Vin, made such a horrible mistake with him. Because of that, she reminded herself, she listened to her head now, not her heart.

More than likely she was mistaken about her emotions. She'd spent and would continue to spend a lot of time with Griffin Devaney. He'd saved her life twice. It only made sense she would feel something for him, but it wasn't a romantic thing. Was it?

It didn't matter. Whatever she felt about him would lead nowhere. She was leaving in a few days and would probably never see him again. She pushed away the disappointment that bit at her.

The silence in the vehicle grew heavy. "So," she said. "What do you do when you're on a stakeout alone?"

"Watch and wait and try to stay awake. It can be pretty boring."

Laura looked up and down the street. Aside

from the one car they'd seen earlier, no one else had ventured out into the frigid weather.

"You probably had to watch plenty when you were a SEAL, right?"

She felt more than saw him tense. Just as she started to back off the question, he said, "There was a lot of waiting, too."

As long as he was willing to talk, Laura wanted to know everything she could. Laying her head back against the seat, she kept her voice casual. "I remember you saying that you once rescued a woman. Did you also guard people like you're doing for me?"

"Sometimes."

The warmth from his body wrapped around her, giving her a sense of security. "Didn't you say that you were hurt on your last mission? That my aunt volunteered at the hospital where you recovered?"

He nodded. "Your aunt is a special lady. She has the biggest heart of anyone I've ever known. Well, until you."

Laura blinked, her pulse scrambling.

"I just mean about forgiveness and…that kind of stuff." He shifted in his seat as if he was uncomfortable. "Uh, maybe the pastor isn't planning to go anywhere tonight. Or to have any visitors."

Clearly, Griffin was ready to change the

subject, but Laura had more questions. For a moment, neither spoke.

"Where are you from?" she ventured.

He slid her a look, his eyes guarded. "A little town in southeastern Oklahoma called Idabel. You've probably never heard of it."

"I have! My college roommate was from there. I visited her a few times. We went to a lake—"

"Broken Bow Lake," he finished.

"Yes. It's gorgeous."

"I spent a lot of time there." There was a hint of sorrow in his voice.

"Do you ever go back?"

"No."

Laura tried to picture him as a boy or even a young man, but she couldn't. All she could imagine was the quietly handsome man with the tortured eyes, as if he'd seen and lived through things she would never understand.

"Why did you choose the military?"

"It was a way out."

"Of Idabel?"

"Of foster homes."

"Oh." She couldn't contain her surprise. "What happened to your parents?"

"My mother died when I was born. I don't know who my father is. I'm not sure she did, either."

"You have no other family?"

"No."

Laura saw no reason to dwell on that sadness. "Was the military what you hoped?"

"I didn't know what to expect." He shrugged. "I wasn't disappointed, I guess."

"And that's where you met your teammates?" She half expected him to shut down the way he had that day at his house when she had asked him about the picture.

"We were all in the same BUD/S class."

"BUD/S?"

"Basic Underwater Demolition/SEAL training." He dragged a hand down his face. "What about you? Did you grow up in Oklahoma City?"

"Yes. Made all of my mistakes here, too, but you already know about those."

Laura let him change the subject. He'd lost his teammates. She couldn't really blame him for not wanting to talk about it. Maybe she shouldn't have asked so many questions, but she liked him. And admired him.

The man had nearly been shot today and his matter-of-fact handling of the shooting, his purposeful decision making had calmed her. Laura wanted to know more because even though he'd answered her questions, he hadn't given any real detail.

Just as he started to take another sip of coffee, he paused. She followed his gaze out the windshield. The lights on either side of the pastor's garage came on and the garage door rattled as it began to go up. The rain had stopped altogether, leaving the driveway wet and glistening.

Laura's muscles tensed as she waited to see if there was a motorcycle inside. First she saw the tail end of a silver sedan, then— There it was! A motorcycle.

Griffin reached into the backseat for the camera and zoom lens he'd brought. "Well, well."

No kidding, Laura thought. Rick Hughes wasn't who she had believed him to be at all and his deceit had anger spiking inside her.

Instead of mounting the bike or getting into the silver car, the pastor walked to the edge of the garage and stood just inside, as if he was waiting for someone.

Griffin snapped a couple of pictures.

Laura glanced over. "Whether he owns that motorcycle or not, he had access to one during the time someone shot at you."

"Looks that way."

In her mind, she'd already concluded the pastor's guilt, but not Griffin. He didn't seem ready to make assumptions the way she did.

The hum of an engine and the splash of water beneath tires had her looking over her shoulder to see a car approaching. Despite the jump in her pulse, the automobile might not be going to Hughes's house.

She and Griffin waited in silence, their breath curling into the chill air. The car passed—a taxicab—then pulled into the pastor's driveway. She and Griffin leaned forward at the same time to get a better look.

A slender man about six feet tall stepped out of the cab. A motorcycle helmet was tucked under his left arm. After paying the driver, the stranger walked up to Hughes, who still stood in the garage doorway.

Griffin took several pictures. As the stranger gave something to Hughes, Hughes passed something to the man.

The two shook hands and the visitor walked over to the bike. He kicked up the stand and settled himself on the seat. After starting the engine and letting it warm up for a minute, he pulled on his helmet, revved the engine and drove out of the garage.

As Griffin turned in his seat to take a photo of the license plate, Laura watched the taillight disappear into the frozen night. "Do you think that cycle belongs to Hughes? Maybe he's loaning it out?"

"Maybe. Or maybe he's storing it for that guy." Griffin reached into the side pocket of his door and pulled out a small notebook. "Either way, Hughes had possession of it this afternoon."

"He could've been the shooter," Laura said faintly.

"Or it could've been the other guy. Even Arrico's attorney."

She nodded, trying to reconcile the possibility of the pastor trying to kill Griffin. And her. Impatience jabbed at her. So far all they had were suspicions.

Beside her Griffin scribbled in the notepad.

The pastor's garage door slid down and in a moment, his shadow passed in front of a window next to the front door. Laura blew out a frustrated breath. She and Griffin were no closer to learning the identity of the person who'd shot at him or the person who had tried to stab her with a syringe or attacked her in the ladies' room.

Just as frustrating was the fact that she felt as if she knew more about who might be posing the threats than she did about the man who was protecting her.

SIX

Laura should've been an interrogator. She'd gotten things out of Griffin last night that he'd never shared with anyone.

He still wasn't sure why he'd told her about Emily. The only people he'd ever told about his former fiancée were his dead teammates. They'd known all about her, but that was before she walked away from Griffin because of his PTSD. PTSD brought on by the ambush that had killed his friends. He hadn't shared that with Laura and wouldn't.

Deep down he felt a grudging admiration that she hadn't stopped trying to get answers out of him. Answers he wasn't going to give her, but he did admire the effort. He admired *her*. Too much.

It was one reason he was glad to be away from her for a little while. He had a job to do and thinking about Laura, becoming friends with her, interfered with that. Already she was chipping away at the boundaries he usually had no trouble maintaining.

Admittedly, this case was unlike any he'd worked before and she was unlike any client. Those things were more than enough reason to keep things between them professional.

Two hours after breakfast with Laura, Griffin was in north Oklahoma City to surveil Vin Arrico's attorney. Harlan Thompson's legal firm was on the fourth floor of a towering twenty-story glass building.

The sky was overcast and gray, but the sleet had stopped. The streets were clear though there was ice on some bridges and overpasses. Griffin had originally parked in the far corner of the lot and had seen Thompson arrive alone about forty minutes ago. After he'd gone inside, Griffin sat watching for a space to open up near the man's blue Cadillac sedan. When it did, he backed in so he would have a direct view of his subject.

Under the guise of getting something out of the back of his SUV, Griffin opened the hatch. He stayed low to the ground, slipped over two cars and punctured a hole in Thompson's right rear tire using the combat knife he still carried. By the time the lawyer returned, the tire would be flat.

His face abraded by the harsh wind, Griffin returned to his SUV and slammed the hatch shut. He made himself comfortable in the driver's seat and settled in to wait. Until Thompson showed himself, Griffin would keep himself busy.

He called Boone, then Morales to follow up on information he'd requested from both men last night. At noon he called Laura to touch base with her. He'd given her the burner phone she should use.

"Hello." Her smoky voice put an unexpected kick in his heart.

Surprised at his reaction, Griffin needed a second to catch up. Even Emily had never affected him that way. His job was to check on Laura. That was all he was doing. "Is everything going okay?"

"Yes. Joy and Sydney just arrived at the hospital and I've already texted with Dad. Sydney let him use her burner cell phone to contact me since Aunt Joy couldn't seem to locate hers."

"How is Nolan today?"

"The chemo's making him feel pretty lousy."

Griffin had learned that all of Nolan's cells had to be killed before he could accept Laura's bone marrow.

"But he's a trouper," Laura continued.

"Are things getting easier between you two?"

"I think so. How is your morning going?"

"Not bad so far. I've found out a few things." She had the same inviting way about her as her aunt. Even though he had no intention of sharing anything personal, he felt comfortable talking to her. About most things. "Before I forget to tell you, Boone should be there soon to take you to the clinic for your second injection."

"What did he learn last night about the nurse?"

"Nothing," Griffin said. "She didn't leave her house all night."

"Oh."

The disappointment in Laura's voice tugged at him. "But I got some info from Ghost."

"About the motorcycle rider we saw leaving the pastor's house last night?"

"Yeah. Ghost found the registration on the motorcycle and pulled up a mug shot of the owner. His build doesn't resemble the guy who shot at me and neither did the build of the guy we saw last night."

"So, now what?"

"I'll pay the owner a visit."

"Why?"

"To see if he's the guy we observed last night. Someone could've switched out his license plates."

"Like put on someone else's tag before the drive-by?" she asked.

"Yes. The tag could've been stolen or borrowed. After the shooting, the correct tag could've been put back on."

"Are you going to ask if he let Pastor Hughes borrow his bike?"

"That's one question I have. Ghost is also going to do a thorough search to see if he turns up any connection between the bike owner and Arrico. And also look further into the connection between the bike owner and the preacher."

"Will that take long?"

"Probably not, but I don't know." Griffin knew she had to be impatient for answers. "And I may be here for a while. Arrico's attorney hasn't left his office building since he arrived."

"All right."

"If you want Joy to come back to the house after your injection, just let her know. Sydney can bring her."

"She wants to spend time with Dad and I feel better knowing she's with him. At least one of us can be there."

He nodded, scanning the faces of people walking through the lot to their vehicles. "Boone will let me know when he drops you back at the house, but you might text me, too."

"Will do."

Her voice was subdued and she sounded disheartened. Even though Griffin was doing his job, he felt as if he should do more. Reassure her or something.

Frustrated, he pinched the bridge of his nose.

He wasn't here to hold her hand, although that was what he wanted to do.

Shifting his focus back to the job, he said, "Next time we talk, I'll be able to tell you if Arrico's lawyer has a tattoo or some kind of mark on his left wrist."

"Then we'll at least know if he's the one who tried to strangle me."

"*If* I can place him at the hospital. And bust any alibi he might have."

"Oh. Right. I hope you find something concrete on the attorney today, one way or the other."

"I know waiting for answers is frustrating, but we'll get some."

"Yes, but when? I don't mean to sound unappreciative. It's just—"

"Your time is limited. I know."

"I appreciate your help. I really do."

Her gratitude caused a warmth to spread through his chest.

"I know you're doing everything you can. I just feel like I'm doing nothing sitting here."

"You're donating bone marrow."

"Until then, I feel useless. I can't visit my father. My aunt has to shoulder the entire load of caring for him. This just isn't right."

"No, it isn't."

"I may never see Dad again. It feels like I'm serving a harsher sentence than Vin. He may be in prison, but he can still see his friends and whatever family he has left. I was forced to give up everything and everyone in my life. Yes, I made bad choices and I paid for them, but I feel as if I'll be paying until the end of my life. Or Vin's."

She exhaled, sounding embarrassed at her mini rant. "None of this is your fault. I'm sorry."

"No." Griffin stopped her quietly. "You're due a good gripe. You were ripped out of your world and thrown into a new one. Now it's about to happen again."

"Still, I don't want to sound ungrateful. I appreciate everything you've done for me and my family."

"I know that." He wanted to reach through the phone and take her hand. What was wrong with him? He cleared his throat. "I can't make any promises, but I'm going to do everything I can to tie these murder attempts to Arrico. If that happens, you might have a chance to return home with your own name."

"If anyone can get the job done, I know it's you, Griffin."

She sounded completely certain. Did she know how much her belief in him meant? Not only because they hadn't known each other long, but also because he hadn't been able to get the job done in Afghanistan.

Those men had believed in him, too, and they

had all died. Humbled by her words, he said quietly, "Thanks for that."

"You're welcome."

"Have you already spoken to Yates today?" Griffin asked.

"Yes. He's working on my next identity. I guess that's what set me off."

"That's understandable."

"Thanks for letting me complain," she said quietly.

"Not a problem. By the way, did you say your aunt's phone is missing? Could you check her room and also the blazer she wore yesterday?"

"Yes, I'll do it now."

"Thanks." Several seconds later, after she'd had time to reach her aunt's room, he heard drawers open and close.

Laura came back on the phone. "I've looked everywhere, but I can't find the phone. Now I'm worried. What if it was stolen?"

"We'll find it." Griffin deliberately kept his tone nonchalant. It very well could've been stolen. If it had been taken at the hospital, either the nurse or the pastor could've taken it. But Griffin didn't want to add to Laura's other concerns. "It's probably in the bottom of that giant purse she carries. There could be a truck hidden in there for all we know."

Laura laughed, which was what Griffin wanted. He smiled.

"Ah," she said. "Boone is driving up right now."

"All right. I'll talk to you later."

They disconnected and Griffin stared out at the bank building, its glass glittering in the winter sunshine. She'd said she was fine. She'd sounded fine. But his need to want to confirm that for himself was exactly why he needed distance from her.

He'd been a little surprised by Laura's anger toward Arrico. Not that she felt it. Griffin got that. She truly had given up a lot more than her criminal ex.

But for the first time, Griffin had seen past her poise, seen the fury she must have battled, especially at the beginning of her stint in protected custody. Despite all that he knew about her, he felt as if he'd seen a part of her few people ever did.

Griffin was amazed that it had taken this long for her resentment to surface. Even though afterward she had apologized for complaining.

Was that what having faith did for a person? Helped them handle the bad things in life with a touch more patience or understanding?

Catching a movement from the corner of his eye, he looked up to see Harlan Thompson weaving his way across the parking lot, headed this way. Griffin didn't move, but every muscle tensed as he waited for the man who might have hurt Laura.

In build and height, the attorney resembled the man who had attacked Laura in the ladies' room. Was he also the man Griffin had seen going toward the hospital elevator yesterday with Nurse Inhofe? He hadn't been able to see that guy's face.

Through the window, Griffin heard Thompson curse. He looked over to see the lawyer open the driver's-side door of his sedan and toss in a briefcase. He slammed the door and marched to the slowly opening trunk, where he removed his spare tire along with a jack and wheel wrench.

Griffin pulled a baseball cap low on his head and flipped up his collar. He got out of his vehicle, then walked past the next car and around the hood of the blue Cadillac to the passenger side. That way he would be able to get a quick and easy look at the man's left wrist without being obvious.

Hunching his shoulders against the frigid wind gusting across the parking lot, he asked, "Need any help?"

Thompson barely looked at him. "No, thanks. I've got it."

The attorney fitted the wrench onto one of the lower lug nuts and twisted to loosen the bolt and remove it. He moved on to the next one, then the next, affording Griffin a look at the man's left hand.

There was something there, but it wasn't a tattoo. It appeared to be a birthmark. It was dark and could easily have been mistaken as ink. It also spread to the back of the lawyer's hand. That could easily have been what Laura saw the day she was attacked.

Jacking up his car, Thompson glanced up. "I appreciate the offer."

"You're welcome." Griffin didn't know for sure that Thompson was the person who'd tried to strangle Laura, but he might be. His hands curled into fists and he fought the urge to lay the guy out flat.

Fighting his temper, he turned to walk away. "Hopefully, your day will get better."

"Yeah," Thompson grunted.

Griffin had to force himself to keep going, *make* himself get back into his SUV.

Thompson was now officially a suspect. It didn't mean the attorney was the assailant. It didn't mean he wasn't. Griffin had to prove it one way or the other.

He pulled out of the parking space and drove toward the exit. By the time he left the lot, he had Morales on the phone.

When his friend answered, Griffin bit out, "Can you find out if Harlan Thompson had a court appearance scheduled two mornings ago?"

"Yeah, sure."

"If he didn't, I need you to hack his cell phone records and track his whereabouts using the GPS coordinates. Actually, I want everything you can get on him. Anything."

"No problem. What's going on?"

"What do you mean?" Anger rode him even though he'd tried to slough it off.

"You sound...mad."

Griffin *was* mad. So what?

"I don't think I've ever heard you this angry," Ghost mused. "You usually don't get so invested in a client."

His friend's statement drew Griffin up short. Morales was right. Griffin didn't become involved to this extent in his cases.

Slightly stunned, he said nothing because there was nothing to say. He was furious and it was on Laura's behalf.

The admission cooled him off a bit. He knew this had slowly become personal, but when had she begun to matter so much?

In three days, she would go back to some WitSec-manufactured life and Griffin would go back to the tediousness of his. She would be gone for good. And he was glad about that.

He ignored the voice in his head that called him a liar. He had to spend time with Laura; she was his assignment. But he couldn't allow anything, especially his emotions, to interfere with doing his job. All he had to do was keep things professional between them until she was gone.

Laura's disappointment and impatience from her conversation with Griffin still lingered two hours later. All she could do was keep a low profile. The inactivity, the helplessness churned inside her like acid.

Griffin had tried to boost her spirits by sharing what he'd learned so far about the person they had seen leaving Rick Hughes's house last night. They knew that man wasn't the person who'd shot at Griffin, but they didn't yet know if he was the registered bike owner. And there was still the possibility that the preacher was the one who'd fired on Griffin in the parking garage.

A heaviness hung over her. Laura wasn't sure if it was due to the side effects of her second injection a few hours ago or because of Vin. She had no energy, and the tiredness was aggravated by her latest bout of nausea and the soreness in her bones and muscles.

Telling herself not to dwell on the discomfort, Laura's thoughts turned to last night and the time she'd spent with her bodyguard. Griffin Devaney was tight-lipped, but she had managed to get a few things out of him. His hometown, for one, and the bombshell that he had once been engaged.

It was difficult to imagine the self-contained loner getting that close to anyone. What had his fiancée been like? How long had they been engaged?

Questions about the woman who had walked away from an injured man had dominated Laura's thoughts. Although that wasn't the only thing that had stayed with her since Griffin had opened up.

The interest she'd seen in his blue-green eyes still made her heart beat a little faster. It also made her want to know everything about him, especially what had happened with his fellow SEALs. When she had tried to find out, he'd immediately changed the subject, just as he had on her first day here.

Laura got the message loud and clear. Whatever had happened was off-limits and Griffin carried the burden like a scar. She wondered if her aunt knew the story. If anyone did.

If she could stay longer, get better acquainted with him, would he tell her? She would never know. Once she left here, she would probably never see him again. Just as she wouldn't see her father.

She'd been right to think that yesterday's visit would be her last. The separation from him and Joy hollowed her out just as much as it had when she had "disappeared" ten months ago. All because of Vin.

Resentment blazed through her. The longer she was here, the more it enraged her. She would have loved to take out her frustration by running or kickboxing or doing some other exercise, but she barely had the steam to walk around. Her insides felt as if they were on fire.

The slight symptoms she'd suffered yesterday were nothing compared to today. In addition, she battled the anxiety that followed her like a shadow.

She was jumpy, and earlier she'd prayed, asking for guidance. To combat her nerves, she'd called Marshal Yates for their daily check-in. He had offered her some hope. That was what she should focus on.

The soreness in her body made her feel brittle, broken, and the nausea seemed to be getting worse. Lying down on the sofa until Griffin arrived sounded like a good idea. She slowly made her way to the soft suede couch in the living room.

Just as she toed off her shoes, a sudden burst of noise from outside the house caused her to jump. A mini explosion followed from the same area, even louder.

Icy fear paralyzed her. The hairs on the back of her neck stood up. Were those gunshots? They sounded like gunshots.

Heart racing, Laura struggled to stay calm. Maybe the sounds had been caused by tree branches that had been sheared off by the wind. Or something else broken loose by the gusts of frigid air.

Even so, she pocketed her phone and headed across the wood floor, aiming for Griffin's secret room. She listened hard as she walked into the laundry room and pushed the button on the bottom of the clothes rod.

The back of the linen cabinet swung open and Laura started down the stairs, only now realizing she had left her shoes by the sofa. Another emphatic pop-pop-pop jolted her. The wind howled sharply and she could hear the heavy creak and groan of the trees. Forget her shoes.

Motion-triggered lights flashed on as she made her way to the bottom of the staircase. She stopped at the edge of the large room that housed Griffin's computers and security equipment.

Shaking now, she could barely punch in the code that turned off the laser security beams protecting the entrance. The all-clear ding had Laura padding across the dark tile floor to the bank of flat-screen monitors.

Cameras surveilled every inch of Griffin's property. Between the house and the barn beyond, Laura saw movement. Monitor Two showed a man wearing a black ski mask approaching. He moved closer to the back door that led into the living room.

Panic ripped through her. Before she could blink, a noise like a car backfire cracked the air. Louder than the first noise. Closer. Then she caught the acrid stench of smoke.

She whirled and raced to the vault and the underground shooting range where she would have her pick of weapons and ammunition. Sweat slicked her hands and prickled her neck. Biting back a whimper at the fiery agony in her bones, Laura stopped in front of the steel door with its engraving of the SEAL trident.

She bent to the recessed dark glass panel in the wall so her retina could be scanned. As Griffin had promised, a beep sounded, confirming that he had indeed added her to the system.

She placed her clammy hand on the panel. A different tone buzzed and the vault's bolt snapped open. Heart racing, she glanced over her shoulder as she rushed inside, laboring to pull the steel door shut behind her. She ignored the stings of pain in her arms and legs and moved slowly to the closest of the two walls full of weapons.

She chose the Walther PPK she'd used for practice. At the waist-high cabinet, she opened the third drawer down and grabbed a box of cartridges.

The intruder had to have been sent by Vin. How had he found her? Griffin's home was the one place he could control her security. If someone had tailed him here, he would have noticed and told Laura. He wouldn't have come home until he'd ditched them.

She froze. Aunt Joy's missing burner phone. It held a record of their phone calls and it must have a GPS signal. That had to be how this guy knew her exact location.

Fumbling for her own burner phone, she called Griffin.

"Hey—"

"Somebody's here!"

"On the property?"

"Yes. He was almost to the back door by the time I got downstairs."

"Okay, I'm already on my way. I should be there shortly. Are you in the vault?"

"Yes."

"Locked in?"

"Yes."

"Are you armed?"

"Yes."

"I just took the turn for the road leading to the house."

"Hurry!" Trembling, her muscles burning, she slid down the wall and sat facing the door. She loaded a clip the way Griffin had shown her and shoved it into her gun.

With unsteady hands, she aimed the weapon straight ahead, ready to use it if she had to. Her body throbbed with pain as she tried to breathe through the agony and stay alert.

Laura wasn't sure how long she sat there, but she jerked to painful attention when the door's lock clicked loudly. Pure terror drove through her. Quivering and icy cold, she gripped the gun tighter as the steel door began to open.

SEVEN

Griffin's truck skidded to a stop in front of his house, spraying gravel and dirt. No one was at the front door.

He jumped out, pulling his gun as he raced to the edge of the house. He paused, peering around the corner to make sure he wasn't walking into an ambush. The sudden snick of a lock told Griffin the security bars had been activated. Metal bars slammed down over all the windows and doors.

Griffin took off running and rounded the back of the house in time to see a man making tracks toward the barn and a faded green pickup waiting for him. As the man neared his truck, Griffin debated giving chase but knew he wouldn't reach the barn in time to stop the guy. Besides, he was more worried about Laura.

Sliding his gun into the small of his back, he approached the back door leading into the living room. Smoke puffed out from the pump room. A quick look told Griffin the fire was out. At the living-room door, he punched in a code on the keypad mounted inside the frame and the iron bars shot quietly up into place.

His chest tightened as he went through the laundry room and started downstairs. There were no signs that anything had been disturbed, no signs of foul play. Good.

He went down the stairs two at a time. The instant he set foot in the underground room housing his security equipment, he sprinted across the floor and punched in the vault's override code.

The lock snapped free and he opened the door. There she was, sitting on the floor with a gun pointed straight at him. Relief nearly bowled him over. On reflex he scanned the room, though he knew no one else was there.

Upon seeing him, Laura sagged against the wall. "Griffin," she breathed out shakily.

Not wanting to spook her, he walked slowly toward her. "Are you okay?"

She nodded, still training the weapon on him. The gun wobbled.

He went to one knee in front of her, careful not to move quickly. "You can put the gun down now."

"Someone's here."

"No. He ran off. There's no one else." Griffin

lifted her chin so she would look into his eyes. "I promise."

"How did they find me? Could it have been Joy's burner phone?"

"I think so." Griffin didn't like that, but at least he knew what had become of the missing phone. And now that he was aware, they could take precautions.

"I heard noises. Like gunshots."

"I think it was the water pump shorting out. The intruder probably torched it to create a diversion. You're safe." He eased the Walther from her hand and put the weapon to the side.

She was wan, her mouth pinched white with pain. She shook as if she were in subzero temperature.

"You're hurting?" He gently moved a strand of hair out of her eyes. "The injection?"

She nodded, moving as if to get up.

"Here." Shifting his weight, Griffin carefully slid one arm beneath her legs and one around her back.

She clutched at his shoulder. "What are you doing?"

"Getting you somewhere more comfortable."

She relaxed against him as he carried her to the black leather sofa and eased her into a sitting position.

She still trembled and all Griffin cared about was helping her. He grabbed a cream-colored throw from the back of his couch and drew it around her as gently as he could. Even so, she winced when his hand brushed her arm.

"How about some ibuprofen?"

"Maybe in a minute." She inched closer as if she didn't want him to move.

That was fine with him. He leaned close, her breath tickling his jaw. "You're still shaking. Do you want another blanket?"

"No," she mumbled.

"Are the side effects supposed to get worse than this?"

"I hope not."

He wished she could stop taking the shots, but that wasn't a possibility. Not one she would consider, anyway.

He drew in her fresh soap scent. "What happened earlier?"

"I heard a loud crack, then another. I came down here and there were more noises. Louder, closer. You said you saw someone."

"A man. Didn't get a good look."

"Did he make it inside the house?"

"No." Griffin explained about the security bars.

He reached across her lap for the remote and pointed it toward the bank of security monitors. "Look at the displays. There's no one on the property now."

She moved her head so she could see the

screens. Her hair brushed the back of his hand and the strands were like silk. He had to make an effort not to lean in. Irritated at himself, he rewound the footage for each camera.

Different views flashed by as he studied the screens. Finally, he saw the man approaching the house and disappearing into the pump room. Because there was no access to the house from there, Griffin hadn't installed mechanized security bars on that door. There was a popping noise, then a small explosion. At the sound, Laura started.

He gestured toward the monitor. "What you heard was the pump blowing a fuse before it ignited."

"I did smell smoke."

He nodded.

Her blue eyes were cloudy with discomfort. "Once I heard the noises, I came down here and called you."

"You followed your instincts, which is exactly what you should've done."

She shifted, which fitted her more snugly under his arm. "Did you find out anything new?"

"We can talk about that in a minute." Griffin liked having her so close. "Can I get you anything? Water? Juice? Crackers?"

"No, thank you." She seemed fragile, weary.

"I feel a little better. Did you speak to the motorcycle owner?"

He nodded, debating about how much, if anything, to tell her. He'd wanted to wait until she was past these symptoms, but she plainly didn't. "There's no connection between him and Arrico. Ghost did find a link between the bike owner and Pastor Hughes. They know each other from the prison ministry at the Oklahoma County Jail and that's the extent of it. Before I headed home, I stopped by the office to run ballistics on the bullets from the parking garage."

"And?" Her gaze fastened on him.

"They matched a registered gun, but it was reported stolen about five years ago and nothing has come up about it since."

"So that's a dead end."

"Yes."

"Did you learn anything else from your visit with the bike owner?"

"I did get something." They were talking about the job, but none of this felt professional to Griffin any longer. Right now, with her delicate shoulder beneath his hand, it felt personal.

"Because he lives in an apartment, he asked Pastor Hughes if he could put the motorcycle in his garage for a few days while he went to visit his mother in Dallas."

Her brow furrowed. "Why didn't he just ride his motorcycle down there?"

"Icy roads south of the Oklahoma border. Our weathermen forecasted the same. We just didn't get it this time."

To say Oklahoma weather was unpredictable was an understatement.

"He left the keys in the ignition in case Hughes needed to move the bike for any reason."

Her eyes widened. "So Hughes very well could've taken the motorcycle out that afternoon."

"Or any other time he chose," Griffin confirmed.

"Maybe we're closing in on the person who tried to shoot you."

"I hope so." Griffin thought she seemed a little more steady, but he wasn't quite ready to let go of her.

He tried to get his mind back on track, focus only on the case.

She glanced up at him, tears welling in her eyes. One slipped down her cheek. "I was really afraid that Vin's goon was going to get to me."

"But he didn't." Griffin thumbed away the wetness, taken with the dewy perfection of her skin. "Lucky for him, because you looked like you knew what to do with that gun."

A faint smile curved her lips. "I had a good teacher."

"Do you think you could've used it if you'd needed to?"

"Absolutely."

"Good." Oddly enough, he felt a flare of pride at that.

"It's all thanks to you." She lifted a hand to his face and Griffin's fingers automatically curled around her wrist.

He meant to move her hand away, but he couldn't make himself do it. Slowly, she leaned toward him and Griffin went still.

She brushed his lips with hers and he lowered his head even as he told himself to draw away. He nudged her closer. The kiss was soft and fiery at the same time, something he had never experienced. And shouldn't be experiencing now.

Somehow he found the presence of mind to break the kiss. There was a flash of hurt in her face before she masked it. "Since I'll be leaving in a little over seventy-two hours, I guess there was no point in that."

"No," he said hoarsely, even though he badly wanted to kiss her again.

"We can't do it again," she said.

"No." That seemed to be all he could say at the moment.

He wanted more, wanted to at least explore what might have been between them, but in a few days she would disappear from his life and into a new one of her own.

Cheeks pink, she looked away. "I think I'm able to walk now."

"All right." Relief mixed with frustration. "Let's get you back upstairs."

She still trembled, but not as violently as before. He rose and held out a hand. She let him help her up, then preceded him to the stairs.

As she moved slowly up the steps, she muttered, "I'm not sorry."

Griffin didn't think he was supposed to hear that. He wasn't sorry, either, even though the kiss had been a mistake.

He wasn't kidding himself any longer. When he'd gotten her phone call about the intruder, his heart had constricted hard. If something had happened to her...

He stopped the thought. She was a client, a job. He had to remember that.

But professional was the last thing Griffin felt when he was with her. Still, that didn't mean he had to act on it.

Never, in any of her relationships, had Laura kissed a man before he'd kissed her.

As shocked as she'd been, she thought Griffin had been more surprised. His face, usually so inscrutable, had been easy to read. He'd felt the connection between them. Even so, both knew it could go no further. Maybe that was why Laura couldn't make herself regret kissing him.

Afterward he'd wanted to put some space between them, and she'd known they should.

She'd napped for a couple of hours and felt much better when she woke. Though she still had some discomfort, she was no longer nauseous, and though her bones ached, they didn't burn as deeply as they had before. She walked into the kitchen. The house was quiet and she wondered if Griffin was downstairs in the Batcave.

She wasn't sure she was ready to face him after planting that kiss on him. Maybe she would just wait for him to come upstairs.

The door from the garage opened and he walked in, his USMC T-shirt and gray shorts soaked in sweat. His gaze crashed into hers. "Hope I didn't startle you."

"You didn't. Not really." She sounded breathless, which she didn't understand. Should she apologize for kissing him even though she wasn't sorry? "You've been running?"

"Yeah." He dragged a forearm across his perspiring forehead. "Got my ten miles in."

Ten miles. Even if she'd liked jogging, Laura didn't think she would've been able to make ten miles. Of course, he was a SEAL. That was probably nothing to him.

He walked over to the sink, grabbed a glass

from the cabinet next to the kitchen sink and filled it with water from the tap. He downed the liquid in about three gulps. He refilled the glass and took another swallow before turning to face her. "Want some?"

"No, thanks."

"How are you feeling?"

"Much better." She couldn't quite meet his gaze. "Cooped up, actually."

"I'd be going stir-crazy." He studied her for a moment. "I was headed to the barn to finish my workout, if you'd like to walk down with me?"

"Yes," she answered quickly, anxious to move, to get out of the house for any reason. "If you're sure I won't be in your way."

"You won't."

They went down the hall past the guest bedroom and then through his room, where Laura had never been. The area was spacious with a king-size bed, a matching tallboy dresser and nightstands on either side of the bed. A navy comforter and a matching valance over the French doors were the only color in the room. Combined with the dark wood, the decor pegged the room as completely masculine.

Laura paused at the French doors then she followed Griffin out. They stepped onto a back porch furnished with four seasoned rocking chairs that looked out on a small pond. Brittle cracked grass edged the water, which glittered like murky glass in the afternoon sun.

Yesterday it had been storming with a brisk north wind. Today it was nearly fifty degrees, the sun was shining and the wind was relatively calm.

Laura smiled. She had actually missed the crazy weather here.

She followed Griffin around the corner of the house to a long attached room. Opening the door, he motioned her to look inside.

"This is where the water pump is kept, along with a propane tank hookup and generator."

"This is just above the Batcave," she said.

He nodded. "That's why the sounds were so loud when the pump shorted out and caught fire. It's fixed now. I worked on it while you were resting."

The smell of smoke lingered in the air. Griffin guided her out the door and locked it. "I just wanted you to know where everything happened earlier. And to tell you that if the power goes out, the generator will kick on."

"Thanks."

"Ready?"

She nodded, walking with him down a path that cut through a pasture of winter-brown grass.

He glanced at her. "I found out that Arrico's attorney has a birthmark on his left wrist and it spreads to the back of his hand. Could that have been what you saw that day?"

"Yes." She tried to rein in her excitement. "Everything happened so fast. All I really got was an impression. So this Thompson fellow could really be the guy who tried to kill me."

"Could be. I had Ghost check his whereabouts during the attack on you at the hospital. Thompson didn't have a case on the docket at the courthouse during that time. Nor was he in his office."

She knew that didn't prove anything, but she couldn't stop a jolt of excitement.

"Ghost also hacked into Thompson's cell phone records to try and use the GPS coordinates to track him, but the phone was off."

"Maybe because he was in the ladies' room at the hospital," she muttered.

"Or maybe because he was in a deposition. Or at a doctor's appointment."

"Or anywhere else he would've had to turn off his phone," she finished, irked by the possibility. At least Griffin had a lead. That was something.

Would she get any answers before she left? Laura tried to temper her impatience, tried to still the frustration sawing at her. "Thanks for letting me know."

"Sure," he said as they started down the hill.

"Joy came back after church to change clothes. She didn't want to wake you."

"She left a note saying Sydney was taking her to the rehab hospital for her volunteer shift. Is that the hospital where she met you?"

"Yeah."

Laura walked briskly to keep up with his long strides. It felt good to be outside. She loved not having to feel on guard every second. "Have you ever gone to church with Joy?" Laura asked.

"No."

"Do you attend anywhere?"

"No." He glanced at her, his eyes guarded. "Do you?"

"I found a church I really liked in Pueblo." They topped a small rise. Laura could see the barn in a clearing ahead. "Guess I'll have to find another one wherever I end up."

She really didn't want to think about her next identity, her next residence. "Did you know the people who lived here before?"

"No." He seemed to relax when she changed the subject. "The seller was an older gentleman who'd just lost his wife."

"And this was a farm?"

"Yes."

"Did all of this land belong to him?"

Griffin nodded as they approached the barn. From several yards away, she could see that the

weathered wood still had a hint of red paint.
The afternoon sun gave the structure an old-
world charm. Double doors slid open to reveal
an interior wide enough to accommodate a vehicle. Or the battle-scarred buckboard wagon
parked along the west wall.

The pitched roof came to a point on both
ends, providing an awning of sorts for the doors
that opened to the loft. A couple of small windows on each side let in the light. The scent of
leaves and grass drifted on the breeze as Laura
and Griffin came to a halt inside the barn. Straw
littered the dirt floor. A sturdy but crude-look-
ing ladder was propped against the wall.

She looked around, taking in the neatly kept
interior, the perfectly placed tools on a pegboard
on the wall. Dust motes floated in the patches of
sunlight. "It's a neat old barn, but it's not high-
tech like your Batcave. You didn't want to get
rid of it when you bought this place?"

"No." He glanced around, a fond look on his
face. "Never even crossed my mind. It's been
standing here in this same place longer than
I've ever lived anywhere. Makes me feel permanent, I guess."

Probably not only because he'd likely been
gone more than he'd been home as a SEAL,
but also because of his childhood spent in foster homes.

"I like it the way it is. I keep it maintained,

like the ladder and the roof, the loft, but mostly I leave it alone."

She could see why. It had a certain charm, a peace about it, away from the hectic pace of most people's lives. As her eyes adjusted to the dimmer light, she spied a worn leather speed bag hanging in one of the stalls. In the opposite corner of that space was a traditional heavy punching bag. A pair of large boxing gloves hung on a wall peg and an aged, beat-up trunk sat below against the wall.

"You have quite a setup down here." She smiled. "Are you a boxer?"

"It's something I do to let off steam."

She had some steam she could have let off right now, if she'd had any strength in her arms. She walked over to the boxing gloves, admiring the brown-and-white faded leather. "You've had these awhile."

"Yeah, they've been around."

Next to her hands, they looked like gorilla mitts.

Griffin walked over to her and knelt, opening the trunk. He pulled out a much smaller pair and handed them to her. The dark gloves were discolored from age. "Here, try these."

"I wish I'd known how to do this when I lived with Vin."

He frowned at the mention of her ex.

"Where did you get these?"

"They were mine as a kid."

And he still had them. Interesting. She grinned when one worn-out glove slipped over her hand.

"I don't think I could keep these on long enough to do any damage. How do you put these on by yourself?"

"You can't. I use gloves with Velcro straps when I'm working out by myself." He tipped his chin toward her hands. "These were the first gloves I had. Got them out of the trash one day after school. Let me lace them."

She turned her hands palm-up and he gathered the strings.

As he worked to unknot the laces, she noticed something on his inner wrist. "What's that?"

"What's what?"

She realized what it was. Her SEAL had a tattoo. "You have a tattoo."

He stopped, just went stone-cold still. Now she could identify that it was a date. "Aug 3."

"Is that your birthday?"

"No." The word was clipped.

Oops—it might've been the birth date of his former fiancée. "The date you became a SEAL?"

"No." Most of his face was in shadow and for a half second he looked…broken. He stood motionless, like an immovable wall. A wall of stifling quiet, intimidation, grief.

She felt it rolling off of him. A muscle in his jaw worked and Laura suddenly realized the story behind the tattoo was something terrible. Something painful, and she was afraid she knew what it was. "I'm sorry. I shouldn't have asked."

Griffin released her soft hands and turned away, staring at the scuffed punching bag in the corner but seeing a sandy, dirty expanse of mountainous terrain. Was he going to do this?

"We were called straphangers," he said hoarsely. "Extra manpower brought in for dangerous situations."

Behind him he felt Laura's unflinching regard. "Primarily, we did special surveillance and recon, taking pictures of hot spots and sending them back to base. All of our work was done in the dark and there were a lot of hours where we just waited and waited, watching the target, watching our backs."

He was really telling her. Was it because he wanted to or because he couldn't stop himself?

"We worked in a small unit, four SEALs. One evening, right before dark, we came upon an old man herding goats. We had to decide whether he was a threat or not. Whether to kill him or let him leave. The deciding vote was mine and I said to let him pass.

"Less than an hour later, we were ambushed

by a group of Taliban. The man had gone straight to them and given away our position."

Laura gasped and he almost stopped. He had never talked about it since that awful day he'd had to notify the families of his friends.

"Those guys—" He stopped, his vision blurring for a moment. "We had to get down the mountainside. It was a sheer drop with rock outcroppings."

Just as if he were back there, he felt the sun blazing down, the sweat trickling in his eyes, slicking his back. He would never forget the sensation of heat searing his lungs, the burn of ever-present sand in his nostrils. "We all laid down cover fire as we tried to get down the side of the mountain to a small cave.

"Davy and J.J. had multiple gunshot wounds. They literally took their last breaths shooting, trying to save my and Ace's lives." The acrid stench of gunpowder was real. And the metallic scent of blood stinging his nose. "Then Ace was hit. Six times. That tough old boot just kept shooting back. Shooting and yelling at me to get out of there."

Griffin's throat tightened. "I put him on my back and kept going. I was only feet away from the cave when a bullet ricocheted off of an overhang. A baseball-size chunk of rock flew off, hit me in the chest and I fell. Landed right on top of Ace."

Laura was silent behind him. Griffin didn't turn around, afraid he might stop. Now that he was telling the story, he *had* to finish. "I knew he was dead. My leg was shattered and I was shot up, but I made it to the cave.

"I knew I wouldn't last long once the sun came up." He'd also realized he was on his own. Completely on his own. They had all been trained to fight, to move as one unit, and Griffin was alone. Just as he had been his entire life.

"Trying to sneak away was suicide, but I decided I'd rather be killed doing that than huddling there like a wounded animal. I made it out, then dropped right off the edge."

She drew in a shuddery breath.

"Turned out to be a good thing, though. An elder and his granddaughter found me, got me to their hut and doctored me up. I wasn't worth much for the first couple of days, but when I came to, I found out that the Taliban had threatened to burn down the entire village if they didn't turn me over. That old man and his family refused."

Griffin shook his head. Even now, he couldn't believe the risk those people had taken for him.

"I knew if I didn't get out of that village, all of those people would die. Between the granddaughter and me, we managed to find enough of a radio signal to send out an SOS. Army rangers came in and got me. They got Ace, Davy and J.J., too."

"It's a miracle you survived." Laura's voice shook. "God had a hand in that."

Griffin didn't see it that way. "We wouldn't have been found out if I hadn't decided to let the old guy live."

"Griffin," she said thickly.

"Two days before, we'd seen a young woman flag down a Marine unit as if she needed help. The second they reached her, she detonated a bomb she was wearing. Even after witnessing that, I didn't want to believe the old man would give us up, especially after letting him live."

To this day, Griffin had nightmares about releasing the goat herder. Thinking and rethinking that decision. He'd never get over it.

"Did the families of those men blame you?"

"No, but they should. It was *my* fault."

She moved to stand in front of him and he could see tear tracks on her cheeks. Gently, with just a brush of her fingers, she touched his face. "Do you know what I see when I look at you? A man who would've died for his friends, who almost did. I'm sure they were willing to do the same for you."

That was an innate understanding every soldier shared. "They still shouldn't have had to pay with their lives."

Talking to Laura made Griffin feel ripped

open. He hadn't felt this raw or rocky since he'd gotten his friends on the chopper to bring them home.

She laid a hand on his chest. "The only person I've ever known with a love like that is God. Besides giving His Son's life for you, He gave you three friends willing to do the same."

Griffin had certainly never thought about it that way. And he wasn't sure he wanted to.

He'd never told anyone close to him what he'd just told Laura. He hadn't known her long, but he knew without a doubt that nothing he'd said about that bleak, brutal day in the Hindu Kush would leave this barn.

Had he told her only because she was leaving? Because he knew there was no chance anything more could happen between them? Griffin had no idea. What he *did* know was that the best thing for both of them would be for her to leave.

EIGHT

Griffin had opened up to her. Even the next morning, Laura couldn't believe he had told her about his friends. The friends she'd seen in that photo on her first day here.

Her throat tightened as she recalled the agony in his voice.

She had held her breath, afraid to move because she didn't want him to stop talking. She wished she'd been able to hold him or touch him, something to let him know someone was there for him.

The self-loathing on his face had broken her heart. By letting the Afghan native go, Griffin had done what he'd thought was right and his friends had paid with their lives.

It was plain the man couldn't forgive himself and didn't see how anyone else could, either. But God could and Laura wished she could help Griffin understand that.

When they had returned to his house, she'd

expected him to pull away or act uncomfortable, but he hadn't, not last night and not this morning. She wondered if he'd ever told his ex-fiancée.

Had she known about that horrible day when she had left him? Was that *why* she'd left him? Laura hoped not. The last thing he needed was someone judging his decision as wrong when he was already struggling to live with it.

She hadn't realized the magnitude of the dangers faced by military men and women on a daily basis. Now she'd had a very small glimpse, which had given her more of an appreciation for what they did.

She rinsed off the last breakfast plate and put it in the dishwasher. Griffin had cooked for her and Joy this morning—toast and omelets. They were the biggest omelets Laura had ever seen. She didn't know how many eggs he'd used for each one, but the man liked eggs. A lot.

Talking around the table had been nice and yet had made her a little sad. It had brought home how much she missed the simple things, like a meal with her family.

Suddenly she was aware that he was waving a hand in front of her face.

"Hey," he said in a low voice. "Earth to Laura."

"Sorry." She smiled into his eyes, getting the same flutter in her stomach she'd gotten upon first seeing him this morning. "I drifted off."

"Did you hear me say that Ghost is coming out to upgrade the encryption on my system and add another layer to my firewall?"

"Do you want me to stay out of sight?"

"No." He backed up against the counter and braced his hands on the edge. His gaze searched her face. "He doesn't know your real identity and he's a friend. He's not a threat to you."

"Won't he think it's strange that I'm staying at your house?"

"Maybe, but even if he does, he won't ask."

"Why not?"

"He operates on need-to-know, just like I do."

"After hearing his name so often, I'd like to meet him if you think it isn't a risk."

"It isn't. I trust him with my life."

Because of their conversation last evening, Laura knew the significance of that. And if Griffin trusted him, Laura could, too. Their gazes locked and she smiled, enjoying his nearness. He smiled, too, which he seemed to have done more in the past twenty-four hours than he had in the whole time since she'd arrived. Aware of her aunt's rapt attention on them, Laura leaned down to close the dishwasher.

"I'll take you for your injection after Ghost is finished." Griffin stepped away, looking out the bay window toward the drive. "Ah, here he is now."

"Oh, good!" Joy walked over to the door

leading to the garage. She opened it and Laura heard the quiet hum of an engine before it shut off. A door slammed and she caught the faint slide of the well-oiled automatic garage door as it closed.

Joy met the wiry dark-haired man as he stepped inside. "Alex!"

When she hugged him around the middle, he switched his faded navy duffel bag to the other hand so he could return the embrace. His black eyes twinkled. "Griffin said you might be here. And that you made blackberry cobbler last night."

She laughed. "I did and I saved you some. I'll bring it to the office."

"Can't wait." Leanly muscled, the other man wasn't as tall as Griffin, but his shoulders were just as broad and he looked every bit as tough. Street tough.

Yet with that olive skin, carved jaw and aquiline nose, the man could've been a model. So, this was the man Sydney didn't like.

He walked over to Griffin and shook hands, his gaze lighting on Laura.

"Hello," she said.

"Hi." His voice was quiet, almost shy.

Joy laid a hand on Laura's shoulder. "Alex, this is my friend Laura Parker. Laura, this is Alex Morales, our computer genius."

He looked slightly embarrassed at Joy's praise.

Laura smiled, extending her hand for a quick shake. "Otherwise known as Ghost?"

"That's me. Nice to meet you." He slid a sideways look at Griffin. "Didn't know you had company. I could've come later."

"No." Griffin shifted, his arm brushing Laura's. "After you told me about the massive computer hack on those US banks, I didn't want to wait for an upgrade."

A look of disgust crossed Alex's handsome features. "The hackers were good."

"From China?" Griffin asked.

"Russia. The amount of information they stole has yet to be fully determined, but it keeps growing. Ready for me to get started?"

Griffin nodded, walking across the wood floor to the laundry room.

Joy patted Laura's back. "Go on down. I'll join you in a minute. You can get to know Alex better."

The man shot Joy a smile, revealing a pair of deep dimples.

"All right." Laura didn't see the point in that, but she kept the thought to herself.

Griffin gave Joy a warning look. "Don't be doing any matchmaking."

The older woman laughed. "Who said I was?"

With a wink, she turned and headed for the opposite hallway and the bedroom she'd been using.

Laura smiled at their visitor. "Would you like a cup of coffee? It's fresh."

"That would be great. Just black."

"All right." She glanced at Griffin. "I'll bring it down."

"Thanks." He gave her a warm smile that she felt all over.

He followed his friend down the stairs and Laura poured two cups of coffee, then headed for the security room. As she stepped across the threshold, her gaze moved to the vault and she thought about the photo behind the door. Now she knew what had happened to the men in that picture.

She handed a cup of the steaming brew to Alex and walked over to pass the other mug to Griffin.

He took a sip. "Perfect. Two sugars, just the way I like it."

"I thought I remembered correctly."

Alex spared them a look, drawing Laura's attention from her bodyguard. The computer expert had rolled a silver metal box the size of a mini refrigerator over by the bank of monitors. That must be the server. He popped off the front plate and removed a small part from the inside.

Griffin explained to his friend that a man had tried to break into his house yesterday. "Could you take a look at my surveillance footage and see if you spot anything that might identify this guy? I haven't been able to find much."

"Sure."

The tap-tap of a woman's shoes had Laura looking toward the stairs. Joy joined them, chic and stylish in a black jacket and slacks with a crisp light blue shirt. "Did Alex tell you that he and I attend the same church? He never misses."

"He didn't tell me." So far Alex hadn't said much to Laura. Alex's dark gaze met Laura's. "Maybe I'll see you there with Joy sometime."

"I'd like that." She sincerely would, but of course, it wasn't going to happen.

He replaced the faceplate of the server and rolled it out of the way.

Joy turned to Laura with a broad smile. "Alex mentors at-risk youth three days a week after school. He teaches them computer skills."

Laura could hear the pride in her aunt's voice.

"So far they've used their powers for good," Alex said wryly. "And not for hacking."

As Alex began clicking away on his keyboard, Joy turned to Griffin. "Pastor Hughes came by Nolan's hospital room and asked me to have you contact him."

"Did he say why?"

"No, just that he really wanted to talk to you." She passed him a white business card and he slid it into his front jeans pocket.

"All right."

Laura wondered if it had anything to do with the motorcycle they'd seen in Hughes's garage.

Griffin's gaze shifted to her. "After your injection, I'll bring you back here then meet with Hughes."

She nodded.

"Joy?" A feminine voice called out from the top of the stairs and Laura recognized it as Sydney's.

Her aunt smiled. "Down here!"

Over at the monitors, she saw Alex's shoulders go stiff. Had he found a problem on the computer or was his reaction caused by the woman making her way to the security room?

Sydney stepped into the room wearing dark slacks and a long burgundy coat. Even though her sensible shoes had only a one-inch heel, she looked svelte and tall.

Green eyes sparkling, the brunette smiled. "Hey, everybody—"

Her gaze landed on Alex and her face closed up. Her stunning eyes went flat.

As Laura, Griffin and Joy greeted Sydney, Laura glanced at Alex.

He responded to the newcomer with a brusque "Hello," his features stone hard and blank. He stared fiercely at the computer screen. From the distinct chill that had invaded the room, it was evident that Alex and Sydney didn't like being in such close proximity.

Laura exchanged a look with Griffin. He shrugged as if to say he didn't know any more than Laura did.

A beep sounded and Alex reached into his slacks pocket to pull out a cell phone. After a quick glance at it, he shifted his gaze to Griffin. "Looks like Thompson has substantial gambling debts and he received a large deposit in his bank account a few days ago."

Laura remembered that Griffin had asked Morales to report anything he found on the attorney as well as the pastor and the nurse.

"How big is the deposit?" her bodyguard asked.

"Seven hundred fifty thousand dollars."

Laura nearly choked. She couldn't imagine making that much money in her lifetime, let alone receiving it as a one-time payment.

"Do you have a date for that deposit?"

"Three days ago."

Laura went still. That was the day she'd nearly been killed in the ladies' room. The look on Griffin's face said he had realized the same thing. As had Joy and Sydney.

Alex didn't appear to be aware of the significance. Griffin had said Alex didn't ask many questions, so it was difficult to ascertain just what the computer genius knew.

Sydney angled toward the stairs. "If it's all

right, I'm going to grab some coffee. Joy, let me know when you're ready to leave."

"I'll come with you," the older woman said.

Laura wondered if Alex was curious as to why Sydney was here for Joy or why the woman was at Griffin's so early in the morning.

She glanced at Griffin. "I'll see you upstairs. Let me know if either of you want more coffee."

"Thanks." Alex looked up from his flying fingers to smile at her.

The man was really too good-looking.

Griffin nodded. Laura was about halfway up the steps when she heard Morales say in a low voice, "If she's got anything to do with the case you're working, I can see why you're so invested in it."

Laura felt her cheeks heat and continued upstairs.

Griffin started up behind her but she heard him call out to Alex, "I'll leave you to it."

"All right." The other man sounded distracted.

Griffin followed Laura into the kitchen. Sydney and Joy sat at the dining table, each nursing a cup of steaming coffee. The brunette kept an eye on the laundry room as if to make sure Alex didn't appear. Tension pulsed from her.

After a long moment, she turned to Griffin.

"Thompson is on retainer for Arrico. Why is the deposit suspicious?"

"Those payments are regular monthly deposits. This is a larger amount on a different date."

"A bonus?" Joy suggested.

"Payment," Griffin said grimly.

Laura stared up at him. "For?"

Griffin scowled. "We know Thompson wasn't on the elevator when you were stabbed with the syringe, but the strangling and the drive-by could've been him."

"The payment is for trying to kill me—and you." Laura swallowed around a sudden lump in her throat.

Griffin laid a hand on her shoulder as a heavy silence charged the air. "The timing fits."

She ignored the glance exchanged by Sydney and Joy. "Are you going to ask him?"

"Not yet," Griffin said. "The guy could tie our hands if he figured out we hacked his account."

"You mean sue you?"

"Or bring some other legal action that would shut us down. We need to handle this the right way."

"Why would Vin pay him before the job is done?" Laura asked.

"Because he knows Thompson will keep trying until it is."

"Oh." Those words made her as sick to her stomach as the second injection had yesterday.

Griffin squeezed her hand, drawing her attention to him. "Hey, I'm not going to let that happen."

There was no mistaking the determination in his voice and he'd managed to keep her alive so far. She nodded.

As if suddenly remembering they weren't alone, he released her hand.

"Finished." Alex appeared in the laundry room doorway.

Joy left her chair to hug him again. Sydney studied her coffee cup.

Griffin motioned to the other man. "I'll walk out with you."

Grabbing his coat and keys, Griffin walked to the door leading to the garage, saying to Laura, "Come out when you're ready."

"I will. Just need to get my coat."

Laura closed the door behind him and stepped back into the kitchen.

"Whoa!" Sydney exclaimed. "What's going on with you and Devaney?"

Laura looked from Sydney to her aunt. "Nothing."

"Something," her aunt interjected. "Something romantic."

Laura shook her head. She had no intention

of telling them about the kiss she and Griffin had shared.

Sydney pushed away her coffee mug and leaned forward. "Oh, yes, something's going on. You can feel the electricity between you two."

Laura hadn't thought it noticeable to anyone but her. "There might be a spark there."

The agent chuckled. "That's like saying the Grand Canyon is big."

"Oh, honey." Joy beamed. "This is wonderful."

"No, it's not."

"Why not?" Joy and Sydney asked in unison.

She tried to keep her voice steady. "There's no future in it. I'm leaving in two days. We agreed to leave things alone."

"*We* agreed?" Sydney asked. "That sounds like Devaney admitted he's interested. Y'all talked about it?"

Laura nodded.

The other woman's eyes widened and Joy's mouth dropped open in surprise.

"What's the deal?" Laura asked, slightly exasperated.

Sydney drummed her fingers on the table. "I've never seen Devaney like this."

"Like what?"

"All soft and…gooey. Like he's interested in a woman."

Didn't his coworker know that he'd once been engaged?

Joy fingered the handle of her mug. "Y'all have gotten close in the last day or two. Maybe shared some things with each other."

He had, but Laura wasn't going to say a word about his last days as a SEAL or anything else.

"In the three years I've known him," Sydney said, "this is the closest I've ever seen him come to a relationship."

"Same here," Laura's aunt said.

"We're not in a relationship."

"Maybe not yet." Joy's eyes lit up.

"Not ever."

"Honey, if you get out of WitSec, it might be worth exploring."

Sydney nodded. "He's a good man. Not a lot of those around."

Laura would dearly love to ask Sydney about the tension between her and Alex, but she knew it wouldn't stop the woman asking questions.

"Getting out of the program is a big *if.* Even if Griffin can tie Vin to the attempts on my life and his, Vin's already proven he can get to me even if he's in prison."

Her aunt's face fell and Laura felt a sharp stab of disappointment as she realized she really wouldn't have a future with Griffin or anyone else.

"Unless Vin is out of the picture permanently,

my future is WitSec." Certainly not with the former SEAL she feared she was developing feelings for.

"I want you to have a future with someone." Tears welled in Joy's eyes. "Even if it isn't Griffin."

"Maybe someday," Laura said, although she didn't believe it.

She was a little unnerved at how quickly Joy and Sydney had determined there was something between Laura and Griffin, but she could see why they had.

There was an ease between them today that hadn't been there yesterday and she knew it was partly because of the story he'd shared with her in the barn.

She realized now that she had started to settle in with him. She couldn't let herself do that, couldn't let herself get caught up in what had happened between them yesterday, because in the end, it wouldn't change anything.

If she's got anything to do with the case you're working, I can see why you're so invested in it.

Ghost's words about Laura hammered at Griffin as he drove her to the clinic. Griffin didn't even try to deny it. She was the first woman since Emily to spark more than a passing interest, but it didn't matter.

He didn't want to start something he couldn't

finish and he knew she didn't, either. Why did he have to fall for a woman who was walking out of his life just as quickly as she'd walked into it? He'd loved one woman who'd chosen to walk away and now he was interested in one whose only choice was to walk away. He wondered if that was what had Laura so distracted earlier in the kitchen. Or was it what he'd told her in the barn? He had spilled his guts, and surprisingly, he didn't feel strange about it. What he did feel was frustrated that he couldn't fix things so the woman could stay in Oklahoma City. So she could stay with him.

She'd talked about God sparing Griffin in Afghanistan. Could that really be true? Did God care enough about him to be active in his life? To intervene in bad situations? To send Laura into his path? If so, she wouldn't be leaving, would she?

What had she said? *The only person I've ever known with a love like that is God. Besides giving His Son's life for you, He gave you three friends willing to do the same.*

Griffin had certainly never thought about it that way.

Strangely, he felt more settled inside than he had since he'd lost Ace, Davy and J.J. As if there was some kind of resolution. Griffin wondered if it was possible to turn over some of the guilt to God.

He had to stop thinking about all this. He couldn't afford to split his focus right now. Some solid information from the pastor would help. What he needed was a lead or piece of evidence that directly linked Arrico to these latest murder attempts, but even if Griffin managed to do that, it would only extend Arrico's sentence. That wasn't enough to keep Laura out of WitSec and it had Griffin grinding his teeth.

He took the Kilpatrick Turnpike to southbound Lake Hefner Parkway. After exiting on Fiftieth Street, he drove west to Portland Avenue. The clinic was located at one end of a string of businesses.

The companies were a collection of individual buildings. With their Tudor facades and stone exteriors, they looked more like houses.

Griffin chose a parking space available in the front. He came around to open Laura's door and hurried her inside out of the cold. They stepped into a waiting area done in calming blues and creams. The receptionist motioned them over when she spotted them. They walked through the door that separated the front desk and exam rooms from the waiting area.

The halls were carpeted with the same commercial-grade carpet as the entrance of the facility, while the exam room floors were a shiny linoleum.

Mary Jo Brooks, the plump silver-haired

nurse who had given Laura her previous injections, met them halfway down the hall. Already dressed in a paper gown and shoe covers, she had a mask hung around her neck. On their first day, she had explained the staff wore shoe covers because their hall floors were carpeted and couldn't be sterilized daily like the linoleum surfaces.

The nurse wore her usual broad smile. "Laura, Griffin, how are you today?"

"Just fine." Laura smiled.

Griffin really liked the older woman. Her perky personality and no-nonsense way reminded him of his third-grade teacher.

Nurse Brooks led them down the hall. "We'll use the back exam room today."

Passing several closed doors, they followed her to the last room on the right.

"Busy today?" Griffin asked.

"Yes." The woman showed Laura into the room, telling Griffin that a mask, gown and shoe covers had been provided if he wanted to go in with the patient.

He decided it would be better to monitor things out here. "Thanks. I'll just wait in the hall."

"All right." The nurse indicated the exam table next to the wall where Laura should wait. "I may not be the one to administer your injection today. I'll try, but we're pretty backed up."

"It's okay."

Griffin noticed that she didn't seem to mind. Laura had told him this had happened yesterday, too. Nurse Brooks had given Laura her first injection but not her second. The older woman backed out of the exam room and closed the door, giving him a wink as she hustled her way down the hall and into another room.

He leaned back against the wall, arms crossed as he observed and listened. The receptionist showed a male patient back into an exam room. A female nurse, middle-aged with short brown hair, exited a room with two vials of blood and disappeared around the corner behind the front desk.

A male nurse, wearing a paper mask and gown, stepped out of a room just to Griffin's left and angled across the hall toward Laura's room. The mask covered most of the man's face, but his brown eyes were visible. The gown came past his knees, revealing a pair of khaki slacks.

He put a hand on the doorknob to Laura's room and glanced at Griffin. "This will just take a minute."

Griffin nodded, bothered by something he couldn't identify.

The man stepped inside and closed the door. The sense that something was wrong nagged at Griffin, but he couldn't quite— Brown shoes! The guy wore no shoe covers!

Griffin lunged for the door and burst into the room just as the man pushed up Laura's shirt sleeve.

Griffin grabbed the man's arm. "Stop!"

"Hey!" The nurse recoiled. "What is your problem?"

"Where are your shoe covers?"

The nurse went rigid and he tried to pull away, but Griffin clamped down hard on the guy's biceps. Laura had frozen on the edge of the exam table, eyes wide with apprehension.

"Shoe covers," Griffin snapped.

"I guess I forgot to put them on."

Griffin yanked the guy's mask down, revealing burn scars on one side of his face. The man wrenched his arm away and Griffin put himself between the stranger and Laura.

"What's going on?" Her voice was sharp with fear.

"What *is* going on?" a feminine voice demanded from the doorway. Nurse Brooks.

Griffin jerked his head toward the stranger. "This guy one of your nurses?"

"No, he is not! How did you get in here?" She started into the room.

"No!" Griffin yelled as the fake nurse lunged for the older woman.

Before he could grab Mary Jo, Griffin knocked the guy into the wall, slamming his face into the textured surface. The woman squealed and jumped back.

"What's in that syringe?" Griffin ripped it out of the man's hand. "Laura, go with Nurse Brooks!"

Just as she leaped from her chair, the assailant swung at Griffin, and the punch glanced off of his jaw. Griffin swung back and heard a bone crack. Blood spurted from the other man's nose.

Griffin reached for his gun at the small of his back.

Laura retreated to the corner.

The man kicked, landing a foot in Griffin's midsection. His gun flew from his hand, skittered off somewhere. Griffin doubled over, then rammed his head into the jerk's stomach. He fell against the wall with a thud. Framed posters on the wall shook. The visitor's chair near the window spun away and cracked against the cabinet that held a sink.

Laura ran across the room and into the hall with the nurse. By this time, several people had gathered there.

"I called the police!" Nurse Brooks shouted.

Griffin advanced on the other man, who was bleeding from the nose. Blood trickled from a cut to his own forehead.

His opponent sneered, whipping out a Ka-Bar knife and slashing at Griffin. He barely managed to avoid the blade, aiming a kick at the man's knee. When the jerk stumbled, Griffin reached under his jeans for his ankle sheath and pulled out his own combat knife.

He advanced, narrowly missing a slice to the arm. He brought his other arm up from below, slamming his elbow into the guy's chin. The other man's knife clattered to the floor. Griffin flattened him against the wall, blade to his throat.

The guy grunted, breathing hard.

Griffin slowed his heart rate, steadied his nerves, just as he'd learned in his training. "Who sent you?"

"I ain't talkin'."

Griffin increased the pressure of the knife until it pricked the skin. A dot of blood appeared. "Who?"

"That ain't gonna work on me. I ain't talkin'."

Griffin didn't ease his hold on the man, but he saw a fear behind the belligerence. This guy was more scared of who'd sent him than he was of Griffin.

Sirens sounded outside and Griffin heard feet pounding down the hallway.

"Police! Step back! Let us through!"

Two black officers, one a female, took in the scene. Griffin held up his hands and backed away, knife in the air.

"Drop the knife!"

Griffin did, using his foot to slide it away

from the fake nurse. He looked toward the policewoman. "That's my gun on the floor."

"You licensed?"

He nodded. "It's in my billfold. I'll get it out when you're ready."

"You're familiar with police procedure."

"Yes, ma'am."

"What happened here?" the female officer demanded.

"I want a lawyer," the assailant said.

"He tried to kill my friend." Griffin nodded his head toward Laura, who stood white faced in the hall, the nurse's arm around her.

The woman, whose name badge read Rydell, scanned the group gathered outside the room. "Anybody else see this?"

"I did," Laura said, her voice shaky.

Nurse Brooks stepped forward. "So did I and it's just like Mr. Devaney said. Miss Parker is here for a special injection and I was supposed to administer it. Instead, I get to the room and this one—" she motioned to the man in custody "—is in here with his own syringe. Never seen him. Don't know him. He does *not* work here."

Rydell's partner, Grissom, his badge said, peered at the man still flattened against the wall. "Name?"

"I want a lawyer."

The lumbering cop frowned. "You got anything to say about what went on here?"

"I want a lawyer."

"All right, then." Grissom handcuffed the assailant.

Griffin pointed to the makeshift weapon where it lay on the floor. "That's the syringe he had. I'd sure like to know what's in it."

Rydell pulled a latex glove from her pocket and slid it on before picking up the syringe. "We'll have it tested."

Grissom's dark gaze took in the bystanders. "We need a statement from everybody. Please wait in the reception area. Nobody leaves until we talk to you."

Griffin stepped up to Rydell. "We're willing to give you any information you need, but Miss Parker must receive this injection today. She's a bone marrow donor and she's in the middle of the process."

The slender black woman looked to the nurse, who nodded in confirmation. The woman nodded.

Rydell glanced at Laura, then back at Griffin. "If the nurse here can give the shot to Miss Parker right now, we'll interview all of y'all last."

Griffin looked over his shoulder at the matronly nurse, who still stood with her arm around Laura.

"Yes, I can do that," she said.

He turned back to the policewoman. "Thank you. We'll be waiting when you're ready for us."

She gave him a thumbs-up and stepped out, going up the hall to meet her partner.

The nurse guided Laura inside. "Do you need a few minutes, honey? I sure do."

"Maybe a few." Laura gave her a wan smile.

Griffin waited until Nurse Brooks stepped out, then moved toward Laura. She met him halfway, walking into his arms. She trembled against him.

"Are you okay?" He was concerned about her lack of color.

She shook her head. "I can't believe that just happened. Thank goodness you realized something was wrong. I would've taken that shot and been none the wiser. He could've killed me."

It had been a close call, Griffin thought. Too close.

"Vin sent him," Laura said fiercely. "I don't care if that guy owns up to it or not."

Griffin held her for a moment longer, reassuring himself that she was really all right, that he'd stopped the guy before he'd hurt her.

Laura stepped back, looking up at him. "What do you think was in the syringe?"

"We're going to find out." But the contents were most likely deadly. He rubbed her arms. "You sure you're all right?"

"Yes. Just shaken up."

So was he, although he didn't want to let on. Good thing he'd had his knife today. More than once, he'd been glad that he still carried it.

Nurse Brooks appeared in the doorway. "Miss Parker, if you're ready?"

"I am." She offered the older woman a shaky smile. "Let's do this."

Griffin's admiration for his undercover witness grew. "As soon as the police finish with us, I'll get you home."

"I can't wait." Neither could he. The sooner he got her out of here, the better.

The next morning, Laura was still shaken up. Yesterday she and Griffin had spent hours with the police, answering questions. In the end, Griffin had asked to speak to Rydell and Grissom's lieutenant, and he'd explained Laura's situation to the man. The lieutenant had called Marshal Yates to confirm everything. Once Griffin's story checked out, he and Laura were allowed to leave. They'd also returned his gun and his knife.

She hadn't slept much last night and she had heard Griffin moving around in the house, so she knew he hadn't, either.

The fact that he had to bring her back to the clinic this morning kept him quiet and steel jawed the entire time they were there. Laura didn't like having to return to the place, either, but because of insurance, they had no choice. Boone and Sydney had joined them today, which made Laura feel better. She knew Griffin did, too.

The visit for Laura's fourth injection went off without a hitch. When they came out of the clinic, the other two Enigma operatives went their separate ways. Once in Griffin's SUV, he turned to Laura.

"I don't like the idea of leaving you at the house alone."

"I'll be fine. If anyone else tries to get in, I know I'll be safe in the vault."

He hesitated.

"If you can get any answers about Hughes, Inhofe or Thompson before I leave, I'd appreciate it."

"All right," he said reluctantly. "I want to know if anything weird happens at the house and I mean anything."

"Yes, sir."

"I'll call you as soon as I've finished. You call me every thirty minutes. Deal?"

"Deal." She hoped he could find something to finally connect one or more of their three suspects to Vin.

"If you want, I'll check on your dad while I'm there."

"Thank you."

As Griffin turned down the gravel road leading to his house, she touched his leg. "Tomorrow's the last time we have to go to that clinic."

"I'm glad, except that also it means you'll have to leave."

He didn't want her to go? Maybe she wasn't the only one fighting her feelings. What would things be like if she could stay? She'd like to find out.

She hated the thought of leaving but tried not to complain further. "Things will be quiet when I'm gone."

He gave her a crooked grin as he pulled into the garage and killed the engine. "Maybe I don't like quiet."

"Maybe?" She laughed. "I'd say you don't. You were as cool as could be after being shot at."

"That's from practice."

His reminder of his time in Afghanistan sobered both of them.

He came around to open her door and help her out. Taking her hand, he led her inside, not letting go of her until she was on the sofa in the living room. "I'll be back as soon as I can."

"I'll be fine." She felt safe here.

Despite everything, she felt safe with Griffin. Once she left, would she ever feel safe again?

Once Griffin reached the hospital, he took the elevator to the seventh floor. Rick Hughes was waiting when he arrived.

The man shook his hand, then gestured down the hall. "There's an empty room the nurse said we could use."

Griffin wondered why the chaplain wanted complete privacy. He followed the bald man into a patient room, keeping his place near the door as Hughes moved farther inside and across the shiny linoleum floor. The tan walls and single-person bed mirrored those in Nolan's room.

The white edge of a clerical collar showed beneath the dark blue sweater Hughes wore today.

Griffin waited until the man halted at the foot of the bed. "What can I do for you, Pastor?"

"I understand you spoke to a friend of mine yesterday." The man stuck his hands in his pockets, then took them out. "Harry Bowman."

At Griffin's silence, Hughes continued, "About the motorcycle he stored in my garage?"

"Yes, that's right."

"He said you thought it might've been used in a drive-by shooting and that you were the target."

Griffin nodded. "In the parking garage here."

"Here! Why would you consider Bowman a suspect?"

"He's done time."

"Does he have a grudge against you?"

"It's likely the job was done for money."

"When was the drive-by?"

"Three days ago."

"I believe Bowman was out of town. I don't think he's your shooter. He knows he'll have to return to prison if he gets anywhere close to something like that."

If he was caught, Griffin thought. "He was a starting point. I had a license plate number and traced it to the owner of the bike. I paid him a visit to see if I could ID him as the person who shot at me."

"But it wasn't him."

"No."

The pastor's brow furrowed. "How did you know his motorcycle was in my garage?"

"I staked out your house." Griffin watched the man's reactions closely.

"You staked—" Hughes gave a sharp laugh. "Did you think I had something to do with the drive-by?"

"I thought it was a possibility."

The man's face tightened. "Why would I shoot at you? When would I have had the chance?"

"That day, when Miss Parker and I were leaving this floor, we ran into you."

"Yes, I remember."

"On my way to the parking garage for my SUV, I saw you going the same direction and also entering."

"Yes, because I parked there." Irritation sparked in his hazel eyes.

"You disappeared from sight and the next thing I know, someone dressed completely in black like you, about your build, drives by on a motorcycle and shoots at me."

"Well, it wasn't me!"

Griffin was inclined to believe him, but he kept that to himself. "I had to check."

"You could've just asked me."

"If you shot at me?"

"Yes. Or even if I had a motorcycle." Hughes must have seen the skepticism on Griffin's face. "Oh, you wouldn't have believed me. Do you believe me now?"

"I'm not sure yet."

"Do you think someone could've gotten into my garage, taken the bike out?"

"It's possible."

"Why would I want to shoot you?"

"Again, money." Griffin had his own questions. "Did you know there was an attack a couple of days ago on a woman in the ladies' room on this floor?"

"What!" The man seemed genuinely shocked and concerned. "Was she hurt?"

"Cuts and bruises." Remembering the raw mark around Laura's throat and the cut at her temple had Griffin battling a white-hot fury. Just as he'd felt yesterday when she'd gone chalk white at the realization that Arrico had not only paid a huge amount of money to have her killed but had sent a man to murder her at the clinic. "It happened the day before someone shot at me."

"And you think the incidents might be related?"

"I do." He saw no reason to also tell Hughes about the syringe incident on the elevator.

"Do you know who was attacked? Why she was attacked?"

Griffin answered only the second question. "That's what I'm trying to find out."

"Did anyone see anything? Have you asked around on this floor? I'd be happy to help you do that."

Griffin believed he would but didn't want the man tipping anybody off. Neither did he want Hughes spreading the story around, though there was nothing he could do about that, short of gagging the man. "I've talked to the people I needed to."

Except Nurse Inhofe and he would visit with her before he left the hospital. He fished his cell phone out of his pocket.

"Would you take a look at a couple of pictures?"

"Of course," the pastor said.

Griffin brought up the photo of Arrico and angled it toward the other man. "Do you know him?"

Hughes hesitated. "He looks familiar, but I don't think so."

Griffin narrowed his eyes. Why had the man hesitated? "His name is Vin Arrico. He was convicted about a year ago on drug and human-trafficking charges."

"I don't know him."

"You sure? He's serving his time at McAlester."

The chaplain took another long look. "I worked there for a few years, but I wasn't full-time. The only way I would know him is if he came to Bible study."

"He might have, but probably didn't act that interested in studying." Arrico's purpose in going would have been to enlist the pastor's assistance and Griffin was starting to believe Hughes hadn't been roped in.

Of course, the man might have been helping Arrico without really knowing. "Did you know Nurse Inhofe when she worked at the prison?"

"No. I did know she'd been employed there, but we never met until I began serving this hospital."

Griffin flipped to another picture on his phone. "This is Arrico's lawyer, Harlan Thompson. Maybe you know him or have seen him around?"

"No."

"He might be the one who attacked the woman in the restroom."

Hughes looked again at the image. "I don't

recognize him. Have you shown the picture to others at the hospital?"

"I plan to."

"Don't forget to ask the patients. Even the ones close to having their transplants are allowed to move around right up until the procedure."

"Thanks for the information."

"Certainly. The day before Nolan started chemo, the nurse and I wheeled him around the halls a couple of times before he was confined to bed. And this is his second stay. He may have seen the man in your picture at some point."

Griffin nodded. When he stopped in to check on Laura's dad, he would show him the picture of Thompson and then speak to Nurse Inhofe.

The pastor had seemed genuinely surprised about the attack on Laura and the drive-by in the parking garage. Maybe he had been. Griffin still wasn't sure if the man was involved with Arrico.

Several minutes later, after Griffin had sterilized a burner phone and given it to a groggy Nolan, he showed him the picture of the attorney. Laura's dad didn't recognize the man and didn't recall seeing him around the hospital.

Griffin thanked him and went in search of Cheryl Inhofe. She was at the nurse's station. A petite olive-skinned nurse smiled at him as she filled out a chart.

The redhead he'd come to see propped one hip against the edge of the crescent-shaped desk. She gave him a big flirty smile. "Hello, Mr. Devaney."

He forced himself to smile in return. "Could I talk to you for a minute?"

"Sure."

He hitched a thumb down the corridor. "Maybe down there."

She nodded and told the other nurse that she would be back in a few minutes. She followed him to where he stopped just outside the waiting room.

Until today Hughes had been a more viable suspect than Inhofe. But in the past hour she and the attorney had risen to the top of the list of Arrico's possible accomplices.

Griffin didn't plan to question her about the attack in the ladies' room. The story Laura had given the nurse afterward was that she had fainted. What Griffin wanted was to see Inhofe's reaction when he brought up Laura being jabbed on the elevator.

"Do you remember the first day Miss Parker was here and you rode in the elevator with us?"

"Vaguely."

"Someone tried to stab her with a syringe."

The nurse's brown eyes widened. "Wow. Why?"

"I'm trying to figure that out."

"Someone tried to stab her? You'd think that would've gotten some notice in such small quarters."

He didn't like the flip tone in her voice. "Whoever it was aimed for her side but missed."

"Does someone have it out for this girl? She can't catch a break."

Griffin noticed how different Inhofe's response was from the pastor's. Hughes had just wanted to help. The nurse assumed Laura was at fault and that someone was out to get her.

Griffin's gaze lasered into Cheryl. "What do you mean?"

"Uh…" He could practically see the wheels turning in her head. "Didn't something else happen? In the ladies' room?"

"She fainted."

"Oh. Right."

Interesting that she would bring up an incident that had never been reported or described as an attack. "Did you realize anything was going on when she was targeted on the elevator?"

"Not until you just told me."

"So, you didn't notice anyone acting strangely?"

"No, but all I cared about was getting off my shift and going home."

"You were the only hospital employee in the group."

"So?" She angled her chin at him.

Carefully gauging her reaction, he said bluntly, "You have access to syringes and drugs."

He caught a spark of…something in her eyes before she glared at him. "So does everyone who works here!"

"Yes, but they weren't on the elevator with us."

"You think *I* tried to hurt her?"

"Just checking the possibilities."

"I had nothing to do with it," she said with an indignant sniff.

"Then maybe you'll be able to help me with something else." He pulled his phone out of his pocket and thumbed to the photo of Harlan Thompson. "Ever seen this guy before?"

He thought he saw the briefest flash of recognition in her eyes before she masked it. "Who is that?"

"Someone who's been seen around here a few times."

"Like after the elevator thing?"

"Mmm." And maybe the ladies'-room thing. Griffin let her draw her own conclusion from that nonanswer.

"I may have seen him around, but I don't know him."

Griffin didn't believe her. "That's what Pastor Hughes said, too."

"Why would you ask him? Oh, I guess he spends almost as much time around here as we employees do."

Griffin studied her face. "Did you know him when he worked at the prison in McAlester?"

"No." Her eyes narrowed. "How did you know I worked there?"

"The pastor. He said he knew you had been employed there at one time." That wasn't a lie. Griffin just didn't answer her specific question.

"Oh." She looked disgruntled.

He cocked his head. "Is it supposed to be a secret?"

"No," she scoffed.

He'd done all he could do here for now. "Thanks for your time."

"Sure." She pursed her lips. "You're not a cop, are you?"

"No, why?"

"Why are you asking all these questions?"

"I'm trying to figure out who attacked Miss Parker in the elevator."

"Is she your girlfriend?"

It was a nice idea and none of the nurse's business. He just smiled and walked away.

He hadn't gotten much, but he knew the nurse was lying about knowing Harlan Thompson. He just had to prove it.

If the nurse was Arrico's accomplice, Griffin was certain as soon as he left here, she would call the convict and tell him about Griffin's questions. The same could be true of the pastor.

Crossing the hall, he found Ghost's number on his speed dial.

"Yeah?" Morales answered.

"Do you still have the cell phone number I gave you for the nurse?"

"Yeah."

"Could you do your thing and track her calls?"

"Sure."

"Thanks. I appreciate it. Could you also check phone records for Rick Hughes?"

"The pastor who used to work at the prison in McAlester?"

"That's him."

"All right. I'll get back to you."

If she contacted Thompson, Griffin would have a link to Arrico. If she called the prison, they probably wouldn't be able to find out who she spoke to specifically, but Griffin was willing to assume it would be Arrico.

The attorney and the nurse could both be Arrico's accomplices. For Laura, Griffin wanted to catch everyone associated with the convict.

Though even if he did, that didn't mean she'd be able to stay in Oklahoma City. And, he realized, he really wanted that.

NINE

An hour later, Laura attempted to call her dad again at the number on the new burner phone Griffin had given Nolan. There was no answer. She tried not to become alarmed, well aware that she was anxious about everything. She knew Nolan still felt puny from his chemotherapy. He was probably asleep, knocked out from pain meds.

A few minutes later, her burner phone rang. The number was from Aunt Joy's missing phone. She or Griffin must have found it. Good. "Hi."

"Listen up," an unfamiliar masculine voice said.

Her stomach dropped. "Who is this? How did you get this number?"

"We've got your father."

"What!"

"We're at the hospital in your dad's room. If you aren't here in thirty minutes, we'll kill him."

Running up the stairs to the kitchen, Laura snatched up her coat and grabbed the first set of keys hanging on the wall next to the garage door. She bolted out into the garage and headed for the second bay and Griffin's extra SUV. "What about traffic? I don't know if I can get there in thirty minutes!"

"You'd better."

She scrambled up into the gray SUV and started the vehicle, then punched the remote button to open the garage door. "Let me talk to my dad!"

There was only a dial tone. Screaming in frustration, she pressed the gas pedal and sent the truck squealing out of the garage. She barely remembered to hit the remote to shut the door.

She tore up the long gravel driveway that led to the main road. The number to Griffin's cell phone was entered into her speed dial. As the truck swerved and bounced, spraying dirt and gravel, she punched the number 1. *Please still be at the hospital*, she prayed.

He answered on the first ring. "Hey, how's—?"

"They've got my dad!"

"What? Who does?"

"Vin's goons!" She tried to speak past the lump in her throat. "They said they were in his hospital room. Did you stop to see my dad?"

"For just a couple of minutes. He was alone."

"The voice on the phone said I had thirty

minutes to get there or they would kill him. Are you still there?"

"No. I left about twenty minutes ago, but I'm turning around right now."

"Thank you." She nearly sobbed in relief. "You'll be able to get to him before I can."

She reached the main road and turned onto the asphalt.

"Laura, did you leave the house?"

"I had to."

"Go back. Now."

"But they said they would kill him."

"I've got this. Go home," he said sternly.

She didn't see how she could. As if Griffin knew her thoughts, he said, "Turn around. I'll take care of him. Stay on the phone with me."

"Okay." Her nerves were raw, her hands shaking. She knew Griffin would handle the situation.

The caller would be expecting her, not an ex-SEAL. She slowed the SUV and turned the vehicle around. An old brown four-door passed her. The first car she'd seen.

"Where are you now?" Griffin asked.

"I can see your driveway. I'm maybe a hundred and fifty yards away—"

Something heavy rammed the back end of the SUV, knocking Laura into the steering wheel, bending her wrist at an awkward angle. She cried out.

"What is it?" He sounded urgent.

"Something just hit the back of the truck." The rearview mirror showed a car closing in fast. The tan four-door. "It's a car! Brown. Old—"

The car slammed her rear bumper hard, causing her to fishtail. Screaming, she tried to correct but couldn't. "Griffin!"

She plowed into the ditch, headed for a barbed wire fence.

"Laura!" Griffin's voice faded as the phone flew out of her hand.

She fought the wheel, trying to get some traction on the rain-soaked ground. The vehicle struck a rut and slid in sickening slow motion down the fence. Barbed wire clawed the sides of the SUV in an earsplitting metallic screech.

The truck bumped over something—a hole or a rock—and flipped halfway onto its side. The momentum snapped Laura's teeth together and hurled her to the opposite door. She screamed as her head smacked the window. The vehicle crashed to a stop, engine still running.

Head throbbing, she lay stunned for a moment. The driver's-side window shattered and glass sprayed her. That door was jerked open.

"Here, I got 'er," a man said.

Hard hands clamped around her ankles and yanked. She kicked as hard as she could, managing to dislodge one hand. Two pairs of hands fastened on her this time, one on each leg. As they dragged her toward them, she managed to snag the cell phone from the floor. She shrieked and struggled and punched with her feet, though she was tiring fast. She knew her efforts wouldn't free her, but she was able to get their grip to loosen slightly, just long enough to stuff the phone into her coat pocket.

Two goons pulled her out, whacking her head on the running board. She hit the ground with a jarring thud. Pain shot through her. Dazed, she lay motionless.

Cursing and muttering, one thug moved up and flipped her onto her stomach, binding her wrists behind her. He rolled her onto her back and the other man latched on to her ankles. The guy at her head caught her under her arms and the two of them picked her up. She began to struggle again, trying to kick the one at her feet.

They moved a short distance, opened the trunk of their car and pitched her inside. As the door slammed, she cried out and began hammering the side of the vehicle with her feet. The car lurched into motion and sped down the road.

Panic nearly choked her, but she tried to stay calm. *Help me, Lord. Please.* She was able to think past the terror flooding her. Griffin had been on the phone with her when she was ambushed. He knew she was in trouble. He would come for her. Reaction set in and she began to tremble.

She just hoped he found her before they killed her.

Laura's scream had turned Griffin's blood to ice.

He had made the first legal U-turn he could and headed home.

Adrenaline blasted through him. He got Boone on the phone and quickly explained what had happened. "I'm only now exiting the highway. I hope you're closer to my house than I am."

"Sydney and I both are."

"Great!" He checked the GPS signal on his stereo display. "I'm tracking Laura's phone. They're headed west of my house. It sounded as if she was putting up a fight, but these injections take a lot out of her. I don't know for how much longer she'll have the energy to struggle."

"Syd and I are on the county line road right now, heading west. What are we looking for?"

"A brown four-door. Laura said it looked old. If you catch up to them, stop them. I don't care how."

"You got it." Boone hung up.

Whoever had lured Laura out of Griffin's house obviously wasn't in her father's room at OU Medical Center. He called Ghost, who agreed to go to the hospital and report back on Nolan.

Griffin narrowed his focus to finding her, refusing to allow the impatience or the urgency that grew out of his anger take hold. Those emotions would make him reckless. He didn't have time for reckless.

Laura didn't know where they were. Or which direction they were headed. Suddenly the car made a sharp right turn, spinning her around. She heard the splash of water. Then the automobile jerked to a halt. She huddled into a ball, straining to hear anything the men might say. When they'd grabbed her, she had gotten only an impression of rough male features. She hadn't recognized either of their voices.

The wind whistled around the car, drafts of cold air pushing into the trunk. She heard what she thought was the groan of a tree. Or a human. She shuddered.

The trunk popped open and the sudden sunlight had her squinting into the glare.

"Get out." The older of the two men popped a stick of gum in his mouth. He waved his handgun at her, motioning her out.

She tried, but with her hands tied behind her all she could manage was to get to her knees.

"Fletch, she needs help." The second man, who looked barely over twenty-one, smirked.

Lank dark hair, highlighted with a red stripe, fell over his eyes.

While he aimed his own gun at her, the man named Fletch gripped her upper arms and lifted her out of the trunk.

She wobbled, then found her footing. Fletch jammed his gun into her side. "Move it."

She did, searching frantically for the best escape route. They were on a deserted country road, slick with red mud from the recent rain. There were small groupings of trees on both sides of the road, a couple of pines that might provide cover.

Why hadn't they already killed her? Was Griffin nearby? She might not have much time left. Teeth chattering from the cold, she yelled as loudly as she could, "Help! Somebody help!"

The younger man laughed. "Nobody can hear you, lady."

"You're surrounded!" A masculine voice boomed. "Drop your weapons!"

The kid's eyes grew as big as quarters. The disbelief on his face would've been comical in another situation.

Laura recognized Boone's voice. It came from behind them, around the corner.

"Do as the man says and lose those guns," Sydney seconded.

Thank goodness they were here. Laura started to turn toward them. Fletch grabbed her arm in a bruising grip then shoved her behind the car. The younger man moved in front of her so she was stuck between the pair of them.

"Last chance," a different male voice said.

Griffin. The fear crushing Laura's chest eased a tiny bit.

Behind her Fletch laughed, lifted up and fired over the back of the car. Gunfire erupted. Bullets hit the car, dinging metal, shattering glass.

Laura didn't know what to do. Slide under the car? Try to roll away? Neither idea sounded the best. She huddled into a ball, making herself as small as possible.

The younger of her two captors moved farther up the side of the four-door, shooting in bursts. Despite the cold, sweat prickled on her neck. The men on either side of her exchanged fire with Boone and Sydney. Laura flinched after each loud crack. She looked again for a place to run, a way to escape. It was a risk. So was staying put. She could be hit by a bullet either way.

Bullets whizzed past. For every round of shots from her captors, Boone, Sydney and Griffin returned fire. Their shots were spaced out, sparse, aimed at the specific area from where Fletch or the other guy fired.

Laura realized they were afraid she would be hit. So was she! How could she let them know where she was?

As soon as her captors began shooting again, she struggled to her feet and ran past them, away from the car and down the road. She knew they would shoot, but they would also give away their position. She had no doubt that Griffin, Boone and Sydney had better aim than the two clowns who had nabbed her.

A round plowed into the ground behind her. Another one burned past her ear. Two more shots cracked the air around her. She threw herself to the ground, flat against the mud.

Abruptly, silence descended. Shattering silence. Even the wind stopped.

"Laura!" Suddenly Griffin was there, bending over to cut off the flex cuffs. His strong arms helped her up and gathered her to him.

She burrowed close, sobbing.

"Are you hurt?"

"No," she choked out. "Just scared."

She lifted her head, seeing his concerned face through watery eyes. "Did you get them?"

He nodded, stroking her hair. "They're dead."

Maybe she shouldn't have been relieved, but she was. She massaged her sore wrists. "Are Boone and Sydney all right?"

"Yes." He kept an arm around her as he turned her around.

Boone and Sydney waved as they walked toward her.

Laura became aware of the red mud slicked all over the front of her coat. "I'm getting you dirty."

He hugged her. "I don't care."

"My dad?"

"He's fine. Ghost checked on him not too long ago."

She breathed a sigh of relief. "Good. I figured those jerks threatened him just to lure me out, but I wanted to know that he's all right. Thanks for sending Ghost to make sure."

Boone walked up ahead of Sydney. "Sorry for shooting so close to you."

"I appreciate y'all coming for me. It took me a minute to figure out you were trying to determine exactly where I was."

"You're safe," Sydney said. "That's what matters."

"Thank you both so much."

The female agent hugged Laura and Boone patted her shoulder. The four of them began walking toward the corner and the vehicles they'd driven. Laura didn't look at the bodies next to the brown four-door.

Sydney glanced over at Griffin. "We called the local cops. They're on their way."

"I guess we'll have to answer all their questions, just like we had to at the clinic yesterday," Laura said.

"Yes, sorry." Griffin put an arm around her shoulders.

She smiled up at him. "I don't mind at all. I'm glad to still be here to answer questions."

"I'm glad, too." His arm tightened around her. "Very glad."

Hours later, after answering questions from detectives and having Marshal Yates explain Laura's situation, this time to Oklahoma City's chief of detectives, Griffin and Laura headed back to his house. On the way, she asked him to stop for groceries so she could fix dinner for everyone.

He shook his head. "I know you're shaken up and need rest after your close call today."

"I am a bit tired, but I really want to do this. There won't be another chance. Tomorrow will be my last day here."

Griffin looked at her dubiously but relented. "All right."

Once they arrived at Griffin's, she worked on dinner while he went to get his SUV pulled out of the ditch and towed to his mechanic to fix any damage. He had told her he planned to stop while in town to see if Ghost had any new information about Hughes, Inhofe or Thompson.

When he finally returned, Laura insisted dinner would wait until he showered. She herself had had a relaxing bath and changed into slacks and a blue sweater. Now she stood in Griffin's kitchen and looked at the huge dinner she'd prepared. To thank him and his colleagues for all they'd done, she had made lasagna.

It would be hard to say goodbye tomorrow.

Even if Griffin was able to link Hughes, the nurse or the attorney to Vin, Laura didn't see how it could help at this late date. However, she would take any help he offered.

Footsteps coming up from the security room alerted her that the others were on their way up to eat. She slid the French bread into the oven to toast and turned as Griffin, Boone and Joy walked into the kitchen. Sydney was close behind, her wild curls down tonight. Laura had invited Alex aka Ghost also, but he'd declined.

The aroma of savory tomatoes, meat and spices filled the air.

Boone sniffed the air appreciatively. "Sure smells good."

Joy walked around Laura to check the top crust of her blackberry cobbler. "It's hard to beat Laura's family recipe for lasagna. She learned to make it from her mom."

Laura smiled at her aunt.

Sydney chose a seat at the table that positioned her to hear most of the conversation with her good left ear. "I can't wait. It looks wonderful."

Laura placed the pan of steaming pasta at the center of the table, then returned with the salad.

The female agent rubbed her hands together,

her eyes glittering bright green. "It's a good thing Devaney agreed to let you go to the store. I have a feeling he didn't have anything in this kitchen except bread."

"And eggs," Laura added playfully.

"Hey!" Griffin said in mock indignation.

It was nice that they were able to joke after everything that had happened today. She needed light.

She urged everyone to sit. Griffin pulled out her chair, then her aunt's.

As he took the end chair next to Laura, he explained that Alex was staking out the nurse's house.

"Earlier he caught her on the security feed entering the prison. He monitored it hoping to get a shot of her visiting with Arrico, but it didn't happen."

Laura tried to temper her frustration.

"The first frame showed Inhofe stepping into the visitation room. Then a guard motioned her over and she disappeared from view. She was gone for the entire time allotted to visitors. There was no more footage of her until she exited the building."

"So there's no footage of her with Vin," Laura said, struggling to keep her composure. Now what?

Boone nodded. "Ah, they met in a place in the prison without security cameras."

Laura looked from him to Griffin. "The cameras aren't everywhere?"

"No." Disgust was plain in Sydney's voice. "Which means a guard or some other prison employee helped them." So they still had nothing that proved Cheryl Inhofe even knew Vin. Disappointed, she shook her head.

Sydney patted Laura's hand. "The nurse has to come home at some point and Ghost will be waiting. If there's the slightest thing to get on her, he'll get it."

"I hope he can." Laura found the female agent's words encouraging. "I'll pray about it."

"So will I," Joy said.

"What about the jerk who tried to inject me at the clinic?"

"Still not talking," Griffin said. "But Officer Rydell left a voice mail that their lab found pentobarbital in the syringe he intended to use."

There was a long moment of silence. Laura couldn't believe just how close she'd come to death again.

But she was alive. That was what mattered.

She looked around the table, telling herself to savor her last hours here. There was a normalcy in sitting there listening to the sound of voices and laughter, the clatter of silverware. She couldn't remember the last time she'd had normalcy. Or dinner with friends. Who knew if she ever would again? After she assumed her new identity, this night would be a memory she would relive again and again.

Her *second* identity. She pushed away the resentment, determined to enjoy the get-together.

The meal passed quickly and Laura had the chance to see how much the Enigma operatives liked working together. They teased and complimented each other, talking about a couple of past cases. Sydney helped Laura clear the table while Joy dished up piping-hot cobbler, then topped it with vanilla ice cream.

Everyone took their dessert and coffee into the living room. She, Joy and Griffin took the sofa. Sydney sat in one of the overstuffed leather chairs flanking the couch and Boone took the other.

Laura wistfully thought back to the evenings she'd spent with her family before the blowup with Dad. Looking around the room, she smiled as Boone told one terrible joke after another. Sydney and Griffin disagreed about movies and her aunt commented every so often.

Feeling a hand on hers, she looked down. It was Joy offering silent support. Tomorrow Laura would finish what she'd come to do, then leave. She would probably never see Boone or Sydney or Griffin again. She hoped she would someday be able to see her aunt and father.

After everyone finished their dessert, Joy and Sydney gathered the dishes and took them into the kitchen. Boone, Laura and Griffin remained at the table and talked about the Thunder, Oklahoma City's NBA team.

Several minutes later, it seemed everyone was ready to call it a night. Sydney slipped on her burgundy coat, Boone rose and patted his flat stomach, putting on the suit jacket he'd removed before dinner. "Thanks for the meal, Laura. It was great."

"I'm glad you liked it." She started to get up and see him out, but he waved her back.

"No need for that. Syd and I will let ourselves out. See y'all in the morning."

"All right." Laura didn't really want to think about tomorrow.

Griffin walked to the fireplace and knelt to pile in some of the wood stacked to the side. He waved as his colleagues left.

Joy went to her guest room to call Nolan on the new burner phone Griffin had provided. That left just Laura and Griffin.

A comfortable silence settled around them. She wanted to stay here and to spend more time with Griffin, but was that smart? Not according to the rule she'd made for herself after the debacle with Vin. Think with your head, not with your heart. She decided she didn't care. This time tomorrow night, she'd be far away and this would all be a memory.

"You're a great cook." He looked at her over his shoulder.

"Thanks," she said softly.

Before long the scent of wood smoke drifted through the room, mixed with the sugary smell of berries and cobbler. He reclaimed his spot on the sofa and toed off his work boots. Stretching out his legs, he rested his stocking feet on the sturdy dark wood coffee table.

He smiled over at her. "Take off your shoes. Get comfortable."

She removed her shoes and, putting her sock feet on the table, she noticed that his were nearly twice the size of hers.

"Did you get a lot of recipes from your mom?"

"Just some special ones, like the lasagna and her chocolate chip oatmeal cookies."

"I'd like to try those."

Lulled by the crackle of the fire and the solid strength of the man beside her, Laura decided she could stay like this for the rest of her life.

She glanced over. Griffin's eyes were shut, his hands folded across his flat stomach. "What's the problem between Sydney and Alex?"

Without opening his eyes, he shook his head. "They're the only ones who know. Neither one has told me."

"They sure don't like each other."

"True. Have you spoken to your dad again today?"

"Before dinner."

"How did it go?"

"It went well. I didn't tell him what happened today either. I'm too afraid it will jeopardize his health."

Griffin nodded.

"At least I'm able to say goodbye before I go into the program this time." The thought of leaving tomorrow put a knot in her throat. "The good thing is we're no longer estranged. Our relationship is so much better. Though I wish I could stay and build on it. I wish I could stay, period."

"I think everyone else does, too."

Laura wondered if that included him. "It bothers me that I'll have to keep up with my dad's condition through Marshal Yates. Although now I at least know he has a condition."

It also upset her that she wouldn't be able to keep track of Griffin at all. She could really fall in love with this guy, so maybe it was a good thing that she was leaving tomorrow. That was a complication she didn't need. Surely her interest in the former SEAL would fade over time.

"I guess that's one of the hardest things about WitSec," Griffin said. "That you can't see family and friends."

"We're 'strongly discouraged.'" She made quote marks in the air. "Floyd told me that only two people in the history of the program have been killed. In both instances, it was because they came out of hiding. Thanks to you, I haven't had to worry about that."

"Much," he said wryly.

"At all," she said. "If it weren't for you, that guy at the clinic would've hurt me. And even though I was grabbed by those goons, you made sure Boone and Sydney reached me before the jerks had a chance to do me any real harm. I was more concerned that you were going to be the one who got hurt. Or worse."

"Hey." He nudged her thigh with his. "I'm still here and I plan to be. Arrico isn't getting to you or me."

Her protector would be safer once she left, but Laura knew not to say it. "I can't believe my time here is already over."

"I guess this is different from your first go-round with WitSec."

"Yes, and leaving is proving to be more difficult than I expected."

"Because of your family?"

"Not just them. I never expected to like you as quickly as I did." Her cheeks heated. "Not just you. I mean, all of you."

The thought of disappearing again was daunting. Depressing. Of course, when she had accepted protection before, she'd been saving her life and hadn't cared about her future as long as she was away from Vin. Now she did care. "I'll pray about it. I need to let go and trust God."

"To keep you safe?" Griffin asked.

"That everything will work out."

He was quiet for a moment, then said, "Maybe I should try that for my—"

Laura waited for him to finish. When he didn't, she prompted, "Try praying for what?"

He shook his head. "I've already gotten some help."

"With what?"

"PTSD."

She put a hand on his arm. He smelled of man and the outdoors. "You have post-traumatic stress disorder?"

"Yes."

"From the ambush?"

He shrugged. "The episodes started after that."

Laura wanted him to continue talking but didn't think she should push. She started to remove her hand, but he placed his bigger one over it, holding hers in place for a second.

When he released her, her heart tilted. "You said you'd gotten some help?"

"Ghost recommended a shrink friend of his. I still talk to him every once in a while."

She searched his face. "It takes a lot of guts to seek help for a problem like that."

"I had to. After I returned from my tour, there were some days I couldn't function."

"Is that one of the reasons your fiancée left?" Laura had heard a lot of family members couldn't handle the unpredictability, and sometimes the violence, of the disorder.

A muscle in his jaw flexed. "Emily left after one of my episodes."

The shame in his voice tugged at Laura's heart. "Did you hurt her during one of them?"

"No. I never touched her, but I scared her."

"How?"

"I went away sometimes." He tapped a finger against his temple. "Up here. I don't remember much of that. I do remember the nightmares and yelling."

"I hate that she left because of something you had no control over."

"Looking back on it, I don't know how much of a part the PTSD played."

"What do you mean?"

"She told me she couldn't deal with that or the fact that I might get deployed again. I think that was just her way of softening the blow that she'd found someone else."

"Good riddance," Laura muttered.

He grinned. "I've forgiven her."

"You have?"

"Thanks to you. Seeing how you and your dad patched things up."

"Good for you! That's a big deal." Her next words were out before she could stop them. "I wish you could forgive yourself for your friends' deaths."

He stiffened, his leg like iron against hers. "I don't see how anybody can forgive that."

His words, painfully raw, fell into the emptiness around them.

"God can," she said quietly.

He shook his head. She wished she could convince him, but it would take time. Time she didn't have.

He rose, stretching to his full height. "I'm going to call Ghost."

"All right."

"We can watch a movie when I get back. There's a collection of DVDs in the entertainment center." He gestured toward the massive fifty-five-inch television on the adjacent wall and its built-in cabinets.

He'd made it clear he didn't want to talk anymore. That was all right with Laura. By this time tomorrow, she'd be in a safe house or on her way to a new home, with a new name. Griffin would be moving on to the next client.

She squelched her loathing at having to leave again and stood. "I'm really going to miss yo— this place."

"Now that I know what a great cook you are, I'm going to miss you, too."

With a laugh, she swatted at him and he snagged her hand, tugging her toward him. His gaze dropped to her lips.

Her breath jammed in her throat. He wanted to kiss her. She wanted him to. "I thought we agreed not to do this."

"This is the goodbye I won't be able to give you tomorrow with all those people around."

They both knew it wasn't a good idea, but it was all they had. All they would ever have. When he pulled her close and kissed her, she kissed him back.

Not too long after, they drew apart and she looked up at him. His blue-green eyes were sharp with emotion, maybe the same emotion rolling around inside of her. Reluctance, resignation. The thought of walking away hollowed out her chest.

She had broken her rule and followed her heart, not her head.

He stroked her cheek. "One doesn't seem like enough, does it?"

"No. But I guess it has to be."

"I wish we'd met under different circumstances."

"So do I." She squeezed his hand. "I don't want to leave and not just because I have to return to WitSec. But because—I think I'm falling for you."

"Same for me. You're the first woman in a

long time who I've cared about. Who I've let myself care about."

"Talk about bad timing." She grimaced.

He had kept one arm around her and the longer he held her, the harder it became to pull away. And to remember why she had to.

With greater effort than she expected, she stepped out of his arms. "If I don't say goodnight now, I don't think I'll be able to."

"Yeah." The stark acceptance on his face made her heart ache. "I get it."

If only things could be different, she thought. But they weren't. Mentally bracing herself, she gave him a quick peck on the cheek and walked away.

She held the memory of their kiss close. That was all they were going to get and she had to make peace with it.

TEN

Laura woke up the next morning ready for her last injection and to donate her stem cells, but she wasn't looking forward to assuming another identity. Or leaving her life *again*. She abhorred the idea of returning to the program, but she knew she had no choice. Leaving WitSec would put everyone she loved in danger and that wasn't an option.

She looked around the bedroom where she had stayed and made sure she had picked up all of her belongings. Her aunt came in, short gray hair coiffed perfectly. Her makeup was fresh and the silver jewelry she wore set off the navy pantsuit and red blouse.

The older woman finished attaching an earring, then moved over to Laura, sliding an arm around her shoulders to hug her. Laura returned the embrace. "Sydney's here, so I'm going to take off. Is there anything you want me to tell your father?"

"That I love him." She wished she could visit with him, but that wasn't possible. Not after everything that had happened.

"Your appointment at the clinic is for ten o'clock this morning?"

Laura nodded.

"I'll see you there."

After a kiss on the cheek, Joy walked out to meet Sydney. Her aunt wanted to be present for Laura's last injection and for the donation procedure. The other woman had to be relieved that this would be the last day she had to stay at Griffin's or depend on Sydney for transportation.

Laura's things were packed. There wasn't much. Several sweaters and tops she'd bought after arriving, along with a couple of pairs of jeans and a pair of slacks. Plus her cosmetic kit. The dark circles under her eyes showed that she'd gotten very little sleep, so she had applied extra concealer.

From the window in her room, she could see the roof of Griffin's barn. The barn where he'd told her about his friends. And where she'd first realized that she could have feelings for this man. Where her admiration of him had deepened.

"Ready?" Griffin's voice came low and quiet from the doorway.

She nodded, giving the barn one last look

before she turned to pick up the suitcase she'd bought when she had purchased the new clothes. Griffin beat her to it, lifting the bag effortlessly, lean muscles flexing in his arm.

She followed him to the garage and when he opened her door, she climbed into the SUV. As they pulled out of the driveway, she took in the U-shaped layout of the ranch house. Nestled in a shallow valley, it was surrounded by bare-branched trees and acres of land.

"You have a really nice place. Thanks for letting me stay."

"You're welcome."

Neither of them spoke again until they reached the highway that would take them to the clinic.

The day was sunny and breezy. With temperatures in the high thirties, the wind was razor-sharp and Laura welcomed the heat in the SUV.

Griffin glanced over. "Have you already spoken to Yates?"

"Yes. We're supposed to call him once the donation is finished."

"Then he'll meet us there."

"That's right." Griffin signaled and crossed into the right lane. "Boone will meet us there, too. Both he and Sydney have agreed to provide backup."

"That's good."

Just as he exited the Kilpatrick Turnpike to

southbound Lake Hefner Parkway, his phone rang. He pushed a button and answered via the Bluetooth coming through the stereo system.

"Devaney?" Alex Morales's voice was gravelly from fatigue.

"Yeah?"

"The nurse didn't get home until early this morning and Harlan Thompson paid her a visit soon after."

Laura's gaze shot to Griffin's.

He hit the button to increase the volume. "And?"

"I have pictures of them together."

"Excellent!" Griffin threw Laura a hopeful look and she smiled, glad for the news but not really sure how much it would help. "Where is the nurse now?"

"She just went into the hospital. Looks like she's working today."

"Great. I'll be by to talk to her again. Can you keep an eye on her until this afternoon?"

"Yes, and I'll send you the pictures I took with my phone. The better-quality ones are on my camera."

"Thanks. I'll meet with you later for the other ones."

"Will do. Also, I didn't find any phone calls between the pastor and Arrico. Or the pastor and either of your other two suspects."

"Okay, thanks."

The men disconnected and Griffin smiled over at Laura. "That's another lead I can follow. There may be something useful in the photos."

"But I'll be gone."

"I know, but I'm not stopping until I connect Arrico to these murder attempts."

"Do you think it will make any difference?"

"If I can take evidence of his involvement to a judge, I can prove he's able to retaliate against you from prison. I think I have a good shot at getting him moved to solitary."

"Would that help?"

"It would cut off a lot of his communication."

"But he might still be able to finish what he started?"

"Maybe, but it would be much more difficult."

"Thank you. I appreciate anything you can do." Even though it would change nothing. For her safety and the safety of those she loved, she'd still have to give up her life.

There were no spaces available in the front, so Griffin chose a spot facing Portland Avenue, perpendicular to the center.

Sydney's silver SUV was in a south-facing slot, as was Boone's black Lexus sedan.

Laura unbuckled her seat belt. "Looks like everyone is already here."

"They must be inside. Don't get out. I'll come to you."

She waited for him to round the back of the SUV. As he came up the side of the vehicle, she saw him pull a Glock from his back waistband and double-check it. She couldn't believe how many different guns he had. He opened the door and before she could move, he flipped up the collar of her black wool coat.

"It's cold out here," he murmured. Even he was wearing his thick sheepskin jacket.

Her jaw brushed his knuckle and she realized that he was still fingering her collar. "Thank you."

Their eyes caught and held for a moment. Laura wondered what he was thinking. His gaze searched her face and she thought he would say something.

Instead, he stepped back, giving her enough room to move out into the brisk north wind.

"Brr!" The frigid air cut her face and she ducked her head into the neck of her coat.

Just as they stepped out from behind the SUV, a gunshot cracked the air. Laura screamed. Another shot ripped past her.

With one arm, Griffin shoved her back and pushed her to the ground, rolling her slightly under the vehicle and covering her body with his. He already had his gun out. "Stay down!"

Securely beneath him, she heard Griffin fire. She felt him shift slightly, probably aiming from a different angle.

Laura's arms were pinned to her sides. All she could do was huddle into Griffin. A bullet hit the concrete beside her, shards of cement flying against her face. His weight crushed her and she tried to remain still.

He lifted up, firing twice in rapid succession. The noise echoed sharply in her ears. A battery of gunfire rained down. Laura flinched.

Glass shattered. People screamed and shouted. She could hear footsteps but couldn't tell from which direction. A car alarm went off, the shrill blare coming from across the parking lot. Griffin and the unseen shooter were still firing.

Where were Boone and Sydney? Laura wondered. Was Aunt Joy all right?

In the far distance, a siren wailed. Inside, she shriveled. This was all because of her. *Please, Lord, protect all of these people. Don't let them be hurt because of Vin.*

Another volley of gunfire erupted. Griffin shoved her even farther under him, then rose on one elbow and fired toward the roof. He shot again. A bullet flew past, grazing the concrete close to Laura's head. Very close.

An abrupt silence descended. She didn't dare breathe.

Griffin stayed still, his head turned in the direction of the gunshots. Laura could feel the tension in his body, the leashed power straining to erupt.

After a few seconds of quiet, there was a sudden onslaught of voices mixed with screams as people left the businesses in the area and came out to see what had happened. Only then did Griffin look down at her.

His mouth was tight, white around the edges. There was both concern and rage in his eyes. "You okay?"

"Yes." His weight was heavy, but she didn't care. "Are you?"

She heard murmurs and cries of alarm. Over them came Boone's voice. "Anybody hurt?"

"Laura's okay," Griffin said.

The words were labored, as if he was short of breath, probably because he'd hit the ground so hard. She'd had the wind knocked out of her when he had pushed her out of harm's way.

"The shots came from the roof." Sydney sounded as if she was several yards away. "We're headed up there."

People ran past. From the corner of her eye, Laura could see feet, a small crowd gathering. Now that her heart rate was slowing down, she became aware of the cold. Sharp frigid air swirled around them, but the sun still shone.

A few seconds later, Boone yelled, "Side clear!"

From her position on the ground, she could

see people milling about the parking lot, hear sirens getting closer.

A moment later, Boone hollered from up high, "Shooter down."

"Sniper's dead, Devaney!" Sydney called out.

"Good." Laura tried to get a full breath. Reaction set in and she began to tremble. Thank goodness Griffin had been with her.

He eased up on one elbow to look at her, his windblown hair falling over his forehead. Sweat dotted his upper lip. His skin looked waxy. "You sure you're okay?"

"Yes. Are you?" She held on for dear life, clutching him around the middle as if she were the only thing supporting him.

She loosened her grip and dragged her hands over his shoulders, patting and squeezing to make sure he was in one piece.

Without any warning, he slumped down on top of her, his eyes rolling back in his head.

"Griffin?" Her voice sounded loud in her ears. "Griffin?"

Something warm and sticky coated her right palm and her heart skipped as she lifted her hand to see. It was blood. Griffin's blood.

"You've been shot!"

Minutes later it was a mass of chaos. People yelling and screaming, cars from the bordering streets stopping to gawk, other drivers honking angrily at them. Laura could smell the bite of gun smoke in the air, still feel the wetness of Griffin's blood on her hand even though she had cleaned it off.

A police car at each entrance blocked access to the parking lot. An ambulance honked its way through the standing traffic and into the lot, the flashing lights a beacon to additional police who were arriving. Two paramedics elbowed their way through the gathering crowd.

Laura was on her knees beside Griffin, applying pressure to the wound.

He put a hand on her leg. "Is anyone else hurt?"

"No."

"Ma'am, can you let us in?"

She rose and let the younger, stockier of the two men have her spot.

"What happened?" the same man asked. His name tag read Adams.

"He was shot. In the shoulder or back—I can't tell."

Adams and the other medic, Durant, backboarded Griffin in order to stabilize him.

Adams unpacked a bag of saline and inserted a needle into the patient's arm. "Has he been conscious?"

"Yes, and woozy," she answered. The cold

she felt in her blood now had nothing to do with the arctic temperature.

The tall lanky Durant nodded to his partner. "Let's get him on the stretcher."

Laura wrapped her arms around her middle. "Do you think he's going to be okay?"

"We'll do the best we can, ma'am," Adams answered, his dark eyes kind.

The EMTs transferred him onto the stretcher, then lifted him into the back of the ambulance. Durant climbed in first with Adams pushing their patient in the rest of the way. Durant moved into the front to drive.

Adams glanced back at Laura. "Are you his wife?"

"No, we're just—"

"You can meet us at Baptist Hospital."

"Please let me go with you!"

"Are you his fiancée?" Before she could answer, Adams motioned her inside. "You can ride in the back if you want."

She started to get into the ambulance and was stopped by a hand on her arm. She looked over her shoulder to see Sydney.

"The cops need to talk to you," the brunette agent said.

"Can they do it at the hospital? He has to go and I really want to go with him."

Sydney looked at Adams. "Is he critical?"

"His vitals are okay, but we don't know the severity of the gunshot. The doctors need to examine him."

"Okay, thanks." She turned to Laura. "Go. I'll take care of it."

"Thank you."

"We'll see you at Baptist."

Laura climbed into the back of the ambulance and pressed against the wall, staying out of the medic's way.

"Do you know his blood type?" Adams asked.

She shook her head. "I don't."

"It's O neg," Griffin said in a scratchy voice.

He was talking, still conscious. That had to be a good sign. The relief Laura felt made her sag against the wall.

The siren screamed and the vehicle rocked onto Northwest Expressway, speeding down the road until it reached the ambulance entrance on the northwest side of the hospital. She stayed out of the way as the EMTs lifted Griffin's gurney out of the ambulance and rolled him into the ER.

"GSW," Durant yelled as they entered the building.

A male and female nurse and a female doctor came running.

"He's stable," Adams reported.

"O negative," Durant added.

The doctor gave a sharp nod. "Let's get him to X-ray, see what we're dealing with."

The male nurse stopped in front of Laura. "Are you family?"

"I'm with him."

"Wait here and one of us will be back out to tell you what's going on."

"Thank you." Teeth chattering, suddenly aware of how violently she was shaking, Laura made her way to one of the chairs along the wall and sat down. Nerves had her getting right back up.

Her mind was a tangle of questions and desperation. Vin had sent the sniper. She didn't know anyone else who would have. Maybe this incident would connect him to the other murder attempts. Could a link be traced now that the sniper was dead? Was Griffin going to be all right? How much blood had he lost? He'd been conscious. That was encouraging.

Tears blurred her vision and she walked over toward the far wall, away from the other people in the waiting area. The heating unit hummed quietly as she stared out the windows frosted from the cold.

He could've been killed.

This was the second attempt on his life. She needed to start her new life—fast. Once she went back into the program, Griffin would no longer be a target. Neither would anyone else.

* * *

Laura was safe. She hadn't been shot or hurt by the sniper. That was all Griffin cared about.

She stood beside his hospital bed. The streaks of dirt and gravel on her black wool coat were from Griffin pushing her to the concrete and out of harm's way. She had tucked her long hair behind her ear and he searched her face and neck for bruises. There were none. She had no cuts, wasn't bleeding anywhere. She was a welcome sight with her flawless rose-and-cream skin.

"I'm okay," she said as he checked her over. "You're the one who was shot."

"I wanted to see for myself that you weren't hurt."

"I'm not, thanks to you. I don't know if the sniper was after me or you, but if it was me, thank you for saving my life again."

"Since he missed me on the bike, he must've given up on the drive-bys."

"Please don't make light of it." She had a pained expression on her face. In the fluorescent light, her eyes were very blue. And concerned.

"Sorry. I really am all right."

"Are you up to talking to the cops?"

He nodded, increasingly aware of the searing pain in his left shoulder. Laura walked to the doorway and motioned someone inside. She hurried to the corner and picked up the remote to mute the television.

A balding chubby man wearing a rumpled black trench coat was the first inside with a dog-eared notebook. Griffin could easily imagine the man chomping on a cigar.

He looked to be about sixty with sharp dark eyes. His gaze took in Griffin's bandage, visible beneath the thin gown provided by the hospital. "I'm Detective Starnes."

A second man came in. This one was a tall rawboned younger man with red hair and a nicely tailored suit. He introduced himself as Detective Chapman.

He walked up the side of the bed to shake Griffin's hand. "May we ask you some questions?"

"Sure."

"We've already interviewed Miss Parker." Chapman smiled over at her, dropping his voice. "And Marshal Yates."

Griffin's gaze shot to Laura and she nodded. So Floyd had told them about Laura being a protected witness. The marshal probably hadn't had much choice with an investigation going on and it was best that the information had come from him.

"The shooter was dead at the scene," the detective continued. "Did you get a look at him?"

"No. He was on the roof. My colleagues,

Boone Winslow and Sydney Tate, should be able to identify him as the shooter. They found his body."

"Yes, we spoke to them," Starnes said. "We asked Miss Parker if she had any enemies and she named Vin Arrico. We're familiar with the family."

"I'm sure you are," Griffin muttered. Probably starting with Vin's father, Donnie.

Chapman rubbed the side of his nose, looking at Laura with unabashed admiration. "I remember your testimony at his trial."

A funny sensation shot through Griffin and he hoped the man's obvious appreciation was for Laura's courage, not her beauty.

The detective brought his attention back to Griffin. "We understand Arrico has been harassing Miss Parker since her first night back."

"*Harassing* is not a strong enough word. He's been trying to kill her."

"He has someone on the outside helping him," Starnes put in. "Any idea who?"

"Nobody I've been able to pin down yet." Which frustrated him no end. With what he had so far on Hughes, Inhofe and Thompson, the cops wouldn't be able to pull any of them in for questioning. If he could tie any of them to the shooting today, that would change.

Chapman flipped through a small notebook

that was filled with neat handwriting before asking Laura, "Your final injection is tomorrow?"

"It will be if the marshal agrees, then the donation of my stem cells."

He turned to Griffin. "I guess your colleagues are handling her protection tonight if you aren't able to."

"That's right." Griffin shifted against the burn of agony in his shoulder. In the background, *The Andy Griffith Show* played on television.

The policemen asked several more questions and made sure they had the correct contact information for Griffin.

He gestured to the chair where his belongings had been laid out. "I have a card."

Laura moved around Starnes, picked up Griffin's sheepskin jacket and brought it to him. He reached in the side pocket and pulled out a business card. "If you have more questions, you can call or come by the office. All of my phone numbers are on there and so is Enigma's address."

"Thanks." The older detective pocketed the card in his wrinkled black trench coat.

Chapman smiled. "I think we have what we need for now, Mr. Devaney. We'll be in touch if we have other questions."

He nodded. If they had questions after tomorrow, Laura wouldn't be here.

The two men had barely walked out when a roly-poly nurse hustled in to check Griffin's bandage. She wagged a finger at him. "Not too many visitors, young man."

"That was police business, Daisy." He'd seen her name tag as he'd been wheeled in.

"Mmm-hmm." The black woman with an angel's face pursed her lips. "There's a United States marshal wanting to come in, but after that you need to rest. If your wound looks good when the doctor returns, you'll be discharged tonight."

"Okay."

Laura smiled. "Aunt Joy will want to visit you before then."

"You may have to run interference for me." Seeing her smile, he realized it was the first time since he'd arrived at the hospital that her face hadn't been pinched with worry and fear.

Yates peered into the room, cowboy hat in hand. Griffin motioned the man inside, but Floyd looked to Daisy before he entered.

"Yes, yes, c'mon," she said, waving him in.

The marshal stepped into the room. "You don't look too bad."

Daisy stopped at the foot of the bed on her way out. "Three minutes, Mr. Marshal."

"Yes, ma'am."

"And you," she pointed to Griffin. "I'm going to want this bed for someone who needs it."

He grinned and looked over to see a faint smile on Laura's face.

As the nurse left, Yates chuckled. "I can't see anybody disobeying her."

His gaze shifted to Griffin's shoulder. "How much damage?"

"None to my tissue or muscle. I was lucky. It could've been much worse."

"We need to talk about transporting Laura."

"I can't leave today!" she exclaimed.

The marshal frowned. "Seems to me this might be the perfect time. This place is crawling with cops. We should use the protection while we have it."

"We never made it into the clinic. I haven't even had my final injection."

"You haven't donated your stem cells?"

"No."

"How will that affect your father's transplant?"

"It shouldn't. His doctor said it didn't have to be performed the same day I donate. He has twenty-four to forty-eight hours to get my stem cells."

Yates fingered his cowboy hat. "Can you do it right now?"

"Not here."

At the man's frown, Griffin said, "It takes a special machine."

"And that's at the clinic," Laura added. "I

might be able to get them to see me today, but I'd really like to make sure Griffin does all right overnight. I don't want to leave until I know he's settled at home. He's taken care of me all this time. I need to return the favor. Besides, it's only one night."

"I don't like it." The man chewed the inside of his cheek. "The safest, smartest thing would be to get you out of here right now. You don't know who Vin will send next."

"Please, Floyd. Just tonight. I didn't come all this way to fail my dad."

"If it helps, my colleagues will be with her 24/7," Griffin said. "Once we leave the hospital, we'll go to my house. Arrico can't get onto my property without the alarms sounding."

After a moment, Floyd nodded. "The director trusted you enough to vouch for you and your ability to protect Laura. I guess that hasn't changed."

"Thank you, Floyd." Laura came over to hug the man.

His hazel eyes found Griffin over the top of Laura's head.

"You call me in the morning and we'll work out our timetable."

Floyd shook Griffin's hand, then said goodbye.

Laura moved to the side of the bed. "I'm going for more coffee. Do you want anything?"

"No, but I would like to apologize."

Her eyes widened. "For what?"

"That I can't do more about stopping Arrico for good."

"You've done everything you can." There was no mistaking the sincerity in her face. "It's not your fault."

That wasn't how it felt. It felt as if he were failing her just as he'd failed his team. "Still—"

"No." She smiled, sadness lurking in her eyes. "You've saved my life more than once. That's worth more than anything else. You've made it possible for me to still help my dad."

She amazed him. He lifted her hand and brushed a quick kiss across her knuckles. "I wish you could stay."

"So do I."

He thought he saw a tear in her eye before she turned to pick up the half-empty coffee cup she'd used earlier.

Her hair swirled around her shoulders like black silk. He knew it felt like silk, too. He wanted to touch it just once more.

Suddenly the cup fell out of her hand. Brown liquid puddled and spread across the floor as she stood frozen.

"Laura?" Griffin's gaze followed hers to the TV. A picture of Arrico and two other men in orange jumpsuits appeared on the screen with a warning crawl across the bottom: "Three men escaped last night from the federal penitentiary in McAlester. Authorities are still searching for them."

Laura made a sound like a wounded animal. "Vin's out. He'll know to come to Oklahoma City. He may already be here!"

She sounded as if she was on the verge of panic. Even in the fluorescent light of the hospital room, he could see how pale she had gone. Her body trembled.

He sat up and held out his hand. "Come here."

She came toward him, fear on her face. He covered her hand with his. "We'll take precautions. Make sure Boone and Sydney know."

Her eyes were huge and desperate as they searched his face.

"The local LEOs will be all over this, too. Looks like the report is several hours old."

Her pulse jerked in her neck.

"We didn't hear about it because we've been busy here. It will be fine. I won't let him get to you."

"I'm worried about him getting to you!"

"Before too long, we'll be home. I imagine he found out from his goon that he can't get into my house. You and your aunt will both be safe."

She nodded, visibly trying to compose herself. "I can't believe he's escaped."

"Even though he knows you're in OKC, he probably doesn't know you're here at the hospital."

"Right. That's right."

He squeezed her hand. "Okay now?"

"Yes, thanks." She left her hand in his for a moment, then pulled away. "I better clean up this mess—"

"I'll do it."

She gave him an exasperated look.

"The wound is in my shoulder. I'm able to get out of bed and I can use my other hand to mop it up."

"I don't know."

"Go on, if you still want coffee."

She hesitated. "I'll walk down to the waiting area and tell the others that you'll be discharged soon. I can pick up coffee on the way and I'll come straight back."

"Sounds good."

"Okay." She waved to him from the doorway and disappeared.

What he'd said seemed to reassure her, although Griffin would feel better once she returned.

Laura made her way down the hall. Nurses hurried in and out of rooms and a custodian mopped the floor in front of the women's restroom. She continued to the waiting area and saw Sydney, Boone and Joy. They all stood when she reached them.

"How is he?" they asked in unison.

"He's doing well. The nurse expects him to be discharged once the doctor examines him."

"I want to see him," her aunt said.

"Can't we all visit?" Sydney asked.

"The nurse said only one or two at a time. She just about ran Marshal Yates out."

Boone nodded. "Sydney and I will wait. You go ahead, Joy."

The older woman smiled a thank-you and joined Laura on the walk back.

"Is he really all right?" her aunt asked.

"Yes."

Joy hugged her. "He saved your life."

"I know. He's pretty good at that." He'd certainly had enough practice.

More than halfway down the hall, Joy stopped in front of the restroom. "I need to make a pit stop."

Laura thought about continuing on for the coffee and meeting her aunt in Griffin's room but decided she'd rather not be alone. Not with Vin on the loose. "I'll wait for you out here."

"I won't be long." The older woman disappeared into the ladies' room and Laura waited for the janitor in the green scrubs to move away from the water fountain. Once he did, she bent over to get a drink.

A hard hand slammed over her mouth and another wrapped around her upper arm in a bruising hold.

"Hi, baby. Been looking for you."

Vin! Laura's knees almost gave out.

With a hand still over her mouth, he jerked her up with his free arm and shouldered his way through a stairwell door that was propped open with a mop bucket.

Laura kicked and flailed, her head snapping back into his face. He moved his hand to her throat and squeezed. And squeezed. Until black spots danced in front of her eyes.

ELEVEN

Griffin looked at the clock for the fourth time in less than five minutes. Laura should've been back by now.

His cell phone rang and he picked it up from the bedside where she had put it for him within reach. Caller ID showed it was Boone.

Griffin answered. Before he could speak, the other man said, "Laura's gone."

His heart kicked hard. *"What?"*

Biting back a groan, he got out of bed and moved over to grab his shirt off the chair. It was a long-sleeved T-shirt. There was no way he could get it on.

"Joy was headed back with Laura. They stopped at the restroom and Laura said she would wait. Joy came out in time to see Laura being pulled into the stairwell."

"By who?" Griffin said through gritted teeth.

"Joy couldn't see, but she's afraid it was Vin.

We heard he escaped from prison with two other men."

"How would he know where—? Maybe the same way the sniper found her today." Griffin tossed the T-shirt aside, tucked as much of the flimsy gown into his jeans as possible and left the room, gun in hand. "I'm coming to you."

"We'll meet you halfway."

Griffin disconnected and jogged down the hall, pain shooting through him. Adrenaline spiked his system and his shoulder burned like fire, but he kept moving. Boone and Sydney stood in front of the women's restroom.

Winslow motioned that this was the spot where Laura had been grabbed.

"Joy?" He kept his voice low as he approached his friends.

"Sent her to call 911."

"Good."

Sydney pointed to a site map on the wall beside the stairwell door. "There's a basement below and three floors above. Arrico can't get very far."

Griffin just hoped Arrico wanted to keep Laura alive for some reason. "I'll go in this door." He looked at Boone. "Get the key to the service elevator and go up to the fourth floor, then work your way down."

The other man sprinted back toward the waiting-and-admitting area.

Griffin motioned Sydney over. "I need you to cover my back."

"You got it. I can't believe I'm asking this, but would you let Boone and me handle it?"

He just gave her a look.

"Right."

Griffin approached the door and slowly pushed down the pressure bar, moving in measured increments in order to give himself a brief amount of time to react if Arrico were right on the other side. He gradually opened the door.

Just as he held up his hand to give the "clear" signal to Sydney, a loud clank sounded from the floor above. Something hitting metal. He heard it again, then a grunt.

There were three clangs in rapid succession. Someone was kicking the door. Laura?

Griffin lunged into the stairwell with Sydney right behind him. He crept to the first turn of the stairs, heard the meaty sound of flesh hitting flesh, then more grunts. He brought his gun up with one hand, ignoring the discomfort in his opposite shoulder.

On the next staircase, he saw a flash of dark hair, then green scrubs. That told him Laura hadn't noticed Arrico before he'd grabbed her. Finally, he saw the man's face.

"Laura!"

"Here—" Her words were cut off as the convict dragged her around to shield him.

"Stay back or I'll carve her up." Arrico's dark eyes were hard, ruthless. Unflinching.

"Let her go. Nobody has to get hurt."

"I *want* somebody to get hurt. I want Laura to get hurt."

A white-hot fury blanked Griffin's mind for a moment. He wanted to throw himself over the railing and body-slam the guy. He could see the convict, but he couldn't see his hostage.

Griffin started up the stairs. "Are you armed?"

"Yes." Arrico began backing away.

"He's got a knife," Laura yelled before her words were choked off again.

Griffin rounded the corner, now able to see Arrico with his back to the wall as he moved up one stair at a time. With a blade to his hostage's throat and one tattooed arm around her middle, he hauled her with him.

Griffin didn't have a clear shot at the jerk. "You're not getting out of here, Arrico."

"As long as she doesn't, either, I'm good."

He could see Laura. Her face was paper white and she had a wound on her neck. The blood was stark red against the paleness of her skin, drawing attention to the mark left behind after she'd been strangled.

Though her gaze was locked on him, he kept his attention on the escaped prisoner. The convict misjudged a step and stumbled, causing Laura to scream and grab at the wall for support. Arrico recovered quickly, lugging her up with him.

Her scream reverberated in the stairwell. The shrill sound triggered a memory of other sounds—gunfire mixed with cries for help.

Griffin blinked, aware of the cold sweat on his neck and hands. No, no, this wasn't Afghanistan. He wasn't on a military mission. This was Laura. He had to protect Laura.

He reached the landing, which put him four steps below Arrico. He had a clean shot and at this range, he couldn't miss.

He tried to corral the rage that blasted through him. "Let her go, Arrico."

"No way. I'm getting out of here and she's going with me."

"That's not happening," said a feminine voice from below them. Sydney.

Arrico's head jerked around Laura's as he spied the female agent on the lower staircase. Gaze darting around, he ducked again behind Laura and half dragged, half carried her up two more stairs.

She clawed at his hand with both of hers, but she couldn't break his hold. She wheezed for breath as Griffin followed, one slow movement at a time.

Behind Arrico, Griffin spotted Boone's legs. It didn't appear as if Arrico had seen the other man yet.

"Covered up top." Winslow's voice was low and steady.

The convict's face flamed, his eyes blazing in fury. He yanked at Laura, pulling her with him back in the direction they'd come from.

"You're surrounded, Arrico." Griffin fought against the images strobing in his mind. Ace, broken and bleeding on Griffin's back. J.J. and Davy trapped in a crevice.

He had to stay focused on Laura.

Arrico stopped with one foot on a lower step, positioning Laura so that her body covered his entire front. He kept his head behind hers.

There was no air in here. Griffin felt as if he couldn't breathe, but he waited. He didn't blink, didn't move. He had waited on a target for days in much worse conditions. There was no way this jerk could outwait Griffin. Arrico would become impatient and make a mistake.

The man's gaze moved frantically, searching. Up the staircase, then down. The closest door. There were no options without Griffin, Sydney or Boone.

Suddenly Arrico yanked Laura's head back, then shoved her down the stairs. "I'll get you sooner or later!"

She stumbled but managed to catch herself against the wall. Finding her footing, she leaped the last two steps and ran. Boone moved at the same time and tucked her behind him.

Arrico threw his shiv and it clattered down to the landing.

Finally, a clean shot. Griffin sighted his target. If he took this guy out, everything would turn out as it should.

Laura could come out of WitSec and live a normal life. If he had killed that goat herder in the Hindu Kush as he should have, his friends would be alive.

He was almost afraid *not* to take Arrico out. If the guy walked, he would go back to prison, where he had already proven he could get at Laura if he knew where she was. He wouldn't stop trying to kill her.

A low hum filled Griffin's head. His finger curled on the trigger. Griffin would be totally justified in killing him. The news had said the escaped felons were armed and dangerous. All of them had been convicted of murder. As long as Arrico was alive, Laura was in danger. She would have to live in the shadows under another assumed name.

His vision narrowed to just Arrico. His breathing slowed as he sighted the bridge of the convict's nose.

"Devaney?" Sydney's voice penetrated the buzz in Griffin's mind.

Arrico put his hands in the air. "I'm not armed."

"Devaney!" Sydney raised her voice.

Griffin snapped out of his fog, his aim true, his grip rock steady. His gaze shifted to Laura and he saw both fear and pleading in her eyes. Boone watched him closely and he could feel Sydney's steady strength behind him.

Something inside Griffin said don't shoot. But he wanted to so badly that long seconds passed before he could make himself take his finger off the trigger.

And the weasel knew it. The gloating look on Arrico's face made Griffin almost squeeze off a round right then. But he didn't.

Sydney moved out from behind him, her gun trained on Arrico. She pushed the convict into the wall face-first, flattening an arm across his back as she searched him for other weapons.

Satisfied he didn't have more, she slipped a pair of flex cuffs on him. Over her shoulder, she said to Griffin, "Joy called 911 and Marshal Yates. He wasn't very far from the hospital when he heard what was going on. They should be here soon."

She nudged Arrico in the side with her Glock. "Start moving."

He did, but not before he found Laura and blew her a kiss. Fear drew her features tight. Sydney marched the prisoner past Griffin, who opened the door into the ER hallway.

He recognized the drawl in Marshal Yates's words as he took custody of Arrico. As soon as the jerk disappeared through the doors, Laura ran down the stairs to Griffin.

Dismissing the fiery pain in his shoulder, he caught her in a loose hug with his other arm. After a moment, he drew back to get a good look at her neck. He spied only the two cuts. "Are you hurt anywhere else?"

"No." Tears had dried on her cheeks. "Is your shoulder all right?"

"I'm fine."

"I know it was difficult for you not to shoot him."

He nodded. Had that been the right decision? "It would've solved your problem."

"I know." Looking conflicted, she laid a hand on his chest. "What you did was right."

He wasn't sure. He was afraid they would both come to regret it.

He and Laura followed Boone out of the stairwell into a swarm of police and medical personnel. Nurse Daisy hovered over him like a mother hen, guiding him back to his treatment room. She announced that everyone who needed to interview him about the standoff could do it at his bedside while he waited for the doctor to check him out.

After reassuring her aunt that both she and Griffin were all right, Laura stayed with him. One by one, she, Griffin, Boone and Sydney answered law enforcement's questions and recounted the events in the stairwell.

After a long while, when everyone seemed to have what they needed, Floyd Yates stopped by Griffin's room. "How are you doing, Devaney?"

"Still set to go home. Just waiting on the doctor." He dragged a hand down his face.

He was ready to get out of here. The walls seemed to be closing in. He kept second-guessing his decision not to take care of Arrico permanently. Because he hadn't, Laura was returning to witness protection. It was harshly real now. She was leaving, just as Emily had.

He'd known all along that she would. It wasn't Laura's fault and yet it still felt as if he were being dumped all over again.

He'd fallen for one woman who had chosen to walk away and now he'd fallen for one who *had* to.

After what had happened with Vin yesterday, Laura was surprised the incident wasn't dominating her thoughts. She had been terrified at first. Then her emotions had changed to anger, then desperation and back to fear.

Angry that the men he'd hired to kill her had failed, Vin had let her know that he would continue to terrorize her. Griffin had been right that her ex blamed her for not being with his father when the old man passed. He'd made that very clear.

She had never known a hate so strong that it felt like a greasy film, impossible to get off. She'd felt it from Vin. He wouldn't stop until one of them died. If she went back into WitSec, he would find out her new name and where she was.

Laura believed him. Just because he hadn't done it yet didn't mean he couldn't.

She hadn't told Griffin everything Vin had said in the stairwell. Her bodyguard had been wounded while saving her from being shot and he'd gotten her safely away from her crazy ex. Griffin didn't really need anything else dumped on him.

He deserved to not worry about her, especially since there was no immediate threat. Still, she wanted to talk to him about her future, with or without witness protection.

She wanted out. On the drive to the clinic, Laura couldn't quit thinking about it. Even though she was fully aware that the way to stop the threats against Griffin and anyone close to her was to disappear again.

But she was tired of Vin controlling her life. She was tired of hiding. Even though she felt selfish to some degree, she also believed she deserved some normalcy. Didn't she? She'd done the right thing by testifying, by helping put Vin behind bars. Did she really have to spend the rest of her life this way?

Reality told her she did. At least for the foreseeable future. Still, she couldn't help but wish.

Aunt Joy had ridden with them today, and when they arrived, Griffin parked, then walked them both in.

Laura received her final filgrastim injection, then was shown into a small room outfitted with an apheresis machine and a chair that could be adjusted for her comfort. She shuddered when she recalled the man who had posed as a nurse and tried to kill her three days ago.

She could see Griffin remembered, too, as he planted himself just behind Nurse Brooks and watched the older woman with narrowed eyes and an intimidating ferocity.

As the nurse slid a needle into Laura's right arm, she explained that her blood would be taken from a vein in that arm. The blood would flow through the apheresis machine, which would remove the stem cells, and then the blood would be returned to Laura through a vein in her other arm.

Before long both lines were inserted and ready to go. As long as Griffin and Joy didn't excite or upset her, they were allowed to stay.

The nurse checked Laura's vital signs. "Were you told that your donation could take up to six hours?"

"Yes."

"All right, then," the older woman said with a smile. "I'll be in and out to check on you."

After Nurse Brooks left, the three of them watched the blood move through one tube to the machine, where it separated out her stem cells, then returned the blood to Laura through the second tube.

"Amazing," Joy murmured.

Griffin nodded in agreement.

Laura was thrilled that she was finally actually doing something to help her father. She smiled and Griffin smiled back, staring into her eyes for a few seconds. His gaze softened before he looked away.

"How's your shoulder?" she asked.

"Not too bad." Laura felt a distance growing between them. It was unavoidable as the time neared for her to leave.

He sat in one of the chairs provided by the center. Sunlight streamed through the window behind him, highlighting blond strands in his hair. Before long she would be saying goodbye to him. It was too easy to feel sorry for herself, so she channeled her thoughts in another direction.

"Griffin, did Boone or Sydney figure out how the sniper knew where to find us yesterday?"

"They found a tracker on Sydney's car. She pulled a print from it and it matches the nurse."

"Nurse Cheryl!" Joy exclaimed.

Griffin nodded. "We haven't found her prints on anything else so she messed up with that tracker for some reason. Maybe she was in a rush."

"Maybe she was afraid she'd be seen hanging around a car that wasn't hers," Laura said.

"Could be."

"So that tracker links her to the sniper."

"Yes," Griffin said, "but the police also have her cell phone records."

"There were several phone calls between her and the sniper. She couldn't deny their connection. She also confessed to having a relationship with Arrico."

"She was the perfect person to keep an eye out for me," Laura murmured.

"And to hurt you," Griffin said. "She was the one who tried to stab you with the syringe on the elevator."

"How did Vin even know I was in Oklahoma City? Or that Dad was in the hospital?"

"Arrico's attorney, Thompson, said that after you disappeared, Arrico didn't believe you were dead so he had people start watching your family.

"When your dad got cancer the first time, Arrico thought you might show up. He convinced Cheryl Inhofe to leave her job at the prison and try to get hired on at O.U. Medical Center."

Her aunt made a sound of surprise. Laura shuddered at how long Vin had been trying to get to her.

"When Inhofe finally got a job at the hospital, she was able to keep tabs on your dad and aunt during his first hospitalization."

"When Dad finished his treatments and there had been no sign of me, Inhofe just kept the job?"

Griffin nodded. "It didn't take any convincing because the salary at the hospital is much better than at the prison."

"So when Dad got sick this time, Inhofe found out and told Vin," Laura realized.

Joy scooted her chair closer to them. "What about the person who attacked Laura in the restroom?"

"Thompson confirmed it was the sniper and that he was also the one who shot at me from his motorcycle."

"Thompson offered all of this information?" Laura's arms ached where the needles were inserted, so she shifted them carefully on the armrest. "Why?"

"He wants a deal for a lesser sentence. There are plenty of charges to file on him. His bank account showed a deposit into the sniper's account for the shooting yesterday. There were separate earlier deposits for the attempts on us at the hospital."

Laura shook her head. "I can't believe this."

Griffin dragged a hand down his face. "The man who tried to kill you at the clinic confessed that it was Arrico who hired him."

"How could I have been so stupid as to get involved with Vin? I never had a clue how bad he was until it was almost too late."

"I don't think anybody knew how bad he was, honey," Joy consoled.

"How did the nurse get the tracker?" Laura wondered. "Is there a store where you can just go in and buy stuff like that?"

"Actually, yes." Griffin smiled, but it didn't reach his eyes. "I'm not sure where it came from, but Thompson said he was the one who bought it and gave it to Inhofe."

"Is that why they were meeting at her house yesterday?"

"It's probably one reason."

"The sniper was already dead by the time Vin grabbed me at the hospital. How did he know where to find me?"

"The nurse and the tracker," Griffin said in an even tone. "Inhofe gave Arrico the same information she'd given the sniper and he was there in time to see the shooting."

"Did he have a car?"

"Yes, from Inhofe."

"Did she also get the scrubs he wore at the hospital?"

Griffin nodded. "She grabbed a pair from the doctors' lounge."

"So the tracker on Sydney's car led him to the clinic."

"Yes," Griffin said. "And from there he followed the ambulance to the hospital and waited."

"Unbelievable." Joy shuddered, patting Laura's hand. "I'm so glad all of this is over, although I'm not ready for you to leave, honey."

Neither was Laura. Another reason she didn't want to leave was that she wanted to know if Inhofe and Thompson would have to pay for what they'd done. It sounded as though they would. "What about Pastor Hughes?"

"Good news there," Griffin said. "Arrico insists he doesn't know the man."

"Do you believe him?" Laura asked.

"He has no reason to lie."

Laura was glad the preacher had been cleared. He visited her father daily and the two men had established a good rapport.

"Is Vin already back in McAlester?" she asked.

Griffin shook his head. "He's headed there now. Yates called earlier to say he had turned Arrico over to the marshals for Oklahoma's central division and they're transporting him."

"Good," she said fiercely.

"What about the other two escaped convicts?" Joy asked.

"They were apprehended this morning and are in the custody of those same marshals."

Her time here had shown Laura how short life was. If she stayed in Oklahoma City, it could be even shorter for the people she loved. That hurt. But it stung just as much that she had no choice but to leave.

She tried to move past the resentment that had hounded her for the past couple of days.

For the remainder of the time, their conversation was filled with local news and the upcoming holiday. Laura hated that she would miss Thanksgiving with her family.

The white-haired nurse came in to check on Laura and determined her donation was complete. After removing the needles, she disposed of them in the biohazard waste container, then took the bag of stem cells to the area where they would be stored until being taken to Nolan.

When Aunt Joy left the room to call Laura's dad, Griffin's phone rang. As he spoke in a low voice, he wandered around the room stopping to look at the posters on the wall soliciting blood donors. One of them explained the process Laura had undergone. Another illustrated how her father would receive the stem cells.

After the brief conversation, Griffin hung

up and turned to Laura. His face was solemn. "Floyd is here."

So, it was time. Laura wasn't ready, but she knew she never would be. Throat tight, she nodded and rose from her chair.

"Laura?" There was no mistaking Yates's drawl.

Her stomach dropped as the lanky marshal appeared in the doorway. "Hi."

"Everything go okay?"

"Yes." She smiled, though she didn't feel like it.

The older man's gaze skipped from her to Griffin, then back again. "We should probably get going."

Joy stepped around Floyd, came toward Laura and grabbed her in a hug. "I hate this."

"So do I," Laura whispered.

"I believe you'll be able to have a normal life one day," her aunt whispered. "I'm going to pray about it."

Laura squeezed the other woman hard, then released her. Handing Laura one of her embroidered handkerchiefs, she took her own and dabbed at her watery eyes. She stepped away and the marshal gave Laura an expectant look.

Before she could move, Griffin put a hand on her arm, looking at Floyd. "Can you give us a minute?"

"Sure thing." Yates nudged Joy out into the hall and followed, closing the door behind them.

Though Laura was glad to have a moment alone with Griffin, she was afraid she might cry. She'd done enough of that, especially regarding a situation that wouldn't change.

The man she'd come to care for drew her in front of him, his gaze searching her face. "Are you going to be all right?"

"Yes. No." Her voice cracked. "I don't know. I couldn't sleep last night."

"Nervous about donating your stem cells?"

"No. All of these stupid thoughts kept running through my head."

He took her hand. "Like what?"

"Like what if I left WitSec? What if I stayed with my dad?" She could feel his disbelief and his protest. "See, they were stupid."

"Laura."

"Don't worry. I'm not leaving the program. I never even really considered it, but it was a nice daydream."

He folded his arms loosely around her waist. "I wish things were different. I wish I could ask you to stay, but it's too dangerous."

"And not just for me."

"Also your aunt and dad."

"And you," she added. "My being gone will take the target off your back."

"Danger, I can deal with."

"But you shouldn't have to." She shook her head. "This is my fight. I can't ask you to take it on long-term. You've been through enough."

Griffin didn't disagree and a part of her selfishly wanted him to argue. Wanted him to insist he would leave everything and come with her. No one had the right to ask such a thing. She certainly didn't.

He couldn't ask her to stay and she couldn't ask him to go. Not only would it be presumptuous of her to think her bodyguard would even consider it—whatever was between them was too new—but she couldn't ask him to leave his life. She knew *exactly* what that meant.

"After everything we've gone through, my life still isn't my life. Vin can still get to me." She couldn't keep the hard edge of bitterness out of her voice. "I *still* have to move to another place. Still have to get a new identity. I can't leave WitSec, because Vin still wants me dead. Will that ever end?"

Griffin stroked a hand down her hair. "I'm not going to stop trying to get something more on him."

He was in her corner. That was something new this time around. Even if it made no difference ultimately.

She blinked back tears. "I like knowing you're on my side, but—"

"It doesn't change anything right now," Griffin said quietly.

"Right." Resentment bubbled up inside her. Just when she'd given up hope that she might open her heart again one day, she'd met Griffin. And now that was over.

Struggling to keep her composure, she stepped out of his embrace. "I'd better go. This isn't going to get easier. I should be taking my own advice and turning it over to God, but it's hard. I want an answer now."

"I want you to know—" He cleared his throat, his gaze locking on hers. "I'm glad we met. I refuse to believe we won't see each other again."

"I hope you're right." She rolled up on tiptoe and brushed a kiss against his cheek.

He gently turned her face to his and kissed her lips. Tears slid down her cheeks.

I love you. But she kept the words to herself. She touched his face, then walked out.

Laura met the marshal at the front door, glad Griffin hadn't followed. It was hard enough keeping her composure when she saw her aunt. Eyes welling with tears, Joy promised she would keep Floyd updated on Nolan's progress and the marshal would pass the information on to Laura.

As Yates drove her away from the clinic, Laura didn't look back. She couldn't. She was doing the right thing. And it felt lousy. She and

Griffin would never know what might have been between them.

WitSec had cost Laura a lot. Today it felt as if it had cost her everything.

TWELVE

He might never see her again. As Griffin stood watching the marshal's sedan drive away, he rubbed his chest, trying to get rid of the hollowness there. The hopelessness in Laura's blue eyes had hit him hard.

It didn't sit well that there was nothing he could do to keep her here. As a SEAL, he'd learned how to improvise in any situation, how to persevere until he got the result he needed. To be proactive.

Besides chasing down the latest lead on Arrico, was there anything else Griffin could do? There was no way to change the final outcome unless Laura's ex was out of the picture permanently. Griffin had lost that chance when he'd let the felon walk out of the hospital stairwell.

More than frustration gnawed at him. There was anger and doubt. Had he made the wrong choice again, just as he had in Afghanistan? He prayed that he hadn't.

Joy walked up beside him, her gaze following the automobile for a moment before shifting to Griffin. "You have feelings for her."

"A lot of good it does." He did have feelings for her, deep permanent feelings.

Her aunt glowed with pleasure. "She has feelings for you, too."

"And we can't follow up on them. It might not ever matter."

"*You're* giving up?" Joy arched a brow.

Griffin frowned. "No, I'm going to do whatever I can. I just don't know if it will be enough."

Joy touched his arm. "Maybe if you ask, God will show you a way."

Griffin didn't see how, but it couldn't hurt. Feeling restless and out of sorts, he started for Enigma's office. He wasn't ready to face the emptiness of his house. As he drove, Joy's advice came back to him.

Maybe he would pray. He felt strange asking for help when it had been years since he'd even thought about God. *It hadn't been years.* Since Laura had come into his life, they'd discussed God more than once.

Her words in the barn came back to him. She'd said God had sent His Son to die for everyone, even Griffin.

He wasn't sure how to start praying, so he

started with Laura, just laid everything out there—her safety, his feelings about her, the ambush in Afghanistan. When he finished, an unexpected peace came over him for a few seconds. Then a very clear feeling that he had just lost the best thing to ever happen to him in this life.

Letting her go hurt every bit as deeply as losing Davy, Ace and J.J. had.

He knew something else, too. God had sent Laura Prentiss to him. She was a gift he wanted to keep.

Even though he had what he needed to connect Arrico to the attempts to murder him and Laura, all it did was keep the jerk in prison. It might be enough to get him moved to solitary, but it might not. Either way, the guy was still a threat to Laura. So she'd had to disappear again.

But this time, Griffin could go with her.

The thought stopped him cold.

What would it mean to go into the program with her? Because of Laura, he knew what leaving his current life would cost. Not only would it be difficult to cut off contact with his friends and colleagues, it would hurt to leave his house and land. Those things belonged to him. Nothing else ever had. The place was his first real home. Could he give all of that up for Laura?

It would be a trade-off, no doubt. But he

was afraid if he let her go now, it would be for always.

And he couldn't imagine his life without her in it.

Griffin called the director of the US Marshals Service to get things going. By nightfall he had a new driver's license with a new name and authorized documents to present to Marshal Yates. Now he could go wherever Laura went. He wanted to go there now.

Street lights glowed along the highway as he drove north from downtown Oklahoma City. Connecting to his phone via his Bluetooth in the SUV, he called Floyd Yates.

"Devaney," the marshal boomed, "I was just fixin' to call you."

"Great minds, I guess."

"What did you need?"

"Laura. I mean, I've decided to go into Wit-Sec with her. If she'll have me. Have you already relocated her? Can you tell me where she is?"

"She's not with me."

His heart kicked hard. "I'm serious. I need to know."

"I'm serious, too. She isn't here."

"What? Where is she?"

It sounded as if the marshal chuckled, but there was nothing amusing here. "I take it you haven't listened to the news in the last hour," the older man said.

"No. Is she all right?"

"She's better than all right. Arrico and the other two prisoners tried to escape en route to McAlester. They wounded one marshal, but the other one killed them."

Griffin was silent for a moment. "All of them?"

"Yes."

"That means—"

"Yes."

Laura was free! "I'm going after her! Do you know where she is?" Before Yates could answer, Griffin realized. "Never mind. I do."

That night, hours after saying goodbye to Griffin, Laura was at the hospital. She was both happy and sad. Her father's transplant had taken place earlier and gone well. The first sign that the stem cells would be growing and developing would show up in a rising white blood cell count. According to Dr. Farmer, it could take anywhere from ten to twenty-one days for that to appear.

And now she could monitor her father's progress in person. The news that Vin had been killed during another escape attempt hadn't quite sunk in, but she had wasted no time getting to the hospital.

It was hard to believe that late this afternoon, she'd been with Floyd on her way to a new life in Kansas.

Tears of joy filled her eyes and she dashed them away. Boone and Sydney were here, as was Aunt Joy. The only person missing was Griffin, and she planned to duck into a room somewhere to call him.

Even though she hadn't been allowed to see her father yet, the mood she shared with her friends outside his hospital room was celebratory.

Joy looked around their little circle. "Who's up for some dinner?"

"I am," Boone said.

Laura was hungry. She had only now realized that she hadn't eaten since breakfast. "That sounds good to me."

"Me, too."

Down the hall, the elevator dinged. As she looked over her shoulder, her heartbeat skipped. Griffin. She spun to face him. He looked great. Healthy and strong and wonderful. Yes, it had been only hours since she'd seen him, but everything in her world was more vivid now. More appreciated.

Everyone turned, welcoming him with a smile. Laura smiled, too, her heart swelling in her chest.

He addressed all of them, but his gaze settled

on her. "Does this good mood mean Nolan's transplant went okay?"

"Yes. It went very well." Joy explained how long they would have to wait before they received the first sign that the new stem cells were growing.

"That's great news." He still hadn't taken his attention off of Laura.

She had to know. "Did you hear about Vin?"

"I did." He moved closer until she could see the stubble of his late-day beard and the warmth in his blue-green eyes.

The now-familiar flutter in her stomach had Laura smiling broadly. "That's something, huh?"

"Yep, something." His gaze traced her face. "I need to talk to you."

"If it's about earlier—"

"It is. I forgot to tell you something."

She frowned.

"When I agreed with you that nothing in your life had changed, I was wrong. I've changed. My feelings for you have changed."

"They have?"

"Ooh," Joy said.

Laura could feel Boone and Sydney smiling, but she kept her attention on Griffin. Gentle hands cupped her elbows. "You might think it's too soon or that we don't know each other well enough, but I love you."

She blinked up at him, her pulse scrambling. "I love you, too."

"Thank goodness." He brushed a kiss on her lips.

She rested her hands on his arms. "When did you know?"

"When I told you what had happened to my friends, but I didn't see a future then. You were only supposed to be here for a week."

She nodded.

"After you left with Floyd this morning, I realized that God sent you to me and I didn't want to give you up."

He wiped away a tear on her cheek.

She watched him closely. "What would you have done about us if Vin were still alive?"

"I'm glad you asked." Griffin pulled out his new driver's license and gave it to her.

She looked down at the photo. It was Griffin, with a different name. "Who's Griffin Dodd?"

"Me."

"What—?" Understanding spread across her face. "You were coming into WitSec with me?"

"That was the plan."

"You would do that for me? Leave your home and your job?"

"You're my family. I couldn't let you go without me."

He kissed her again. "God put you in my life and you put God in mine."

"You really believe that."

"I do."

Her heart felt too small to contain all the joy. "Oh, Griffin. This is wonderful."

"The best part is no more undercover. You've got your life back."

"No." She smiled up at him. "The best part is having you in it."

EPILOGUE

June sunshine brightened the day, the Oklahoma wind calm. The church picnic was in full swing outside of Griffin's barn. Laura and he had become members of the same church Joy and Ghost attended. Two weeks ago, Griffin had accepted the Lord as his Savior.

Laura hadn't thought it possible to love him more, but she did. Since she had left WitSec seven months ago, their time together had been pure delight. And busy.

"Can you give me a hand here?" he asked behind her.

She turned with a smile, still getting a flutter in her stomach the way she had the first time she'd seen him. He gave her a tray of covered uncooked hamburger patties, then picked up another and followed her to the grill.

He had set up a long card table next to the gas grill and she placed her platter there, then took

Griffin's and did the same. He took the first dozen burgers and put them on the fire to cook.

Laura turned to study the people gathered nearby under the shade of several leafy oak trees. Boone and Sydney were here, as was Ghost. He'd brought a petite pretty blonde with him, keeping plenty of space between him and Sydney.

Aunt Joy sat with Laura's father at a table beneath a flowering dogwood. Nolan Prentiss had accepted Laura's stem cells well and was getting stronger every day.

She picked up a plate and filled it with chips, potato salad and a hamburger fixed the way he liked. She touched Griffin's arm. "I'm taking this to Dad."

He winked, adding more cooked meat to the tray. He called out to the crowd, "Burgers are ready!"

There was a mad scramble toward the food. Some of the teens Ghost mentored were convinced to let the older church members serve themselves first.

Even Pastor Hughes was here. Rick had been a frequent visitor to Nolan in the months after his transplant. The two men had become good friends.

Dodging kids and adults carrying plates of food to the tables set up around the barn, Laura made her way back to the grill and the handsome ex-SEAL manning it.

Griffin grabbed her for a quick kiss. "I have a question for you."

"Well done, please."

He chuckled. "It's not about your hamburger."

"Oh." She grinned.

"Now that you're finished with WitSec—"

"Shh." She glanced around. "I thought we weren't going to talk about that in public."

Griffin flipped several charcoaled patties onto a clean platter, then put on more to cook. "You've been through a lot of changes since last November."

"Yes." They hadn't all been easy, either, like trying to reconnect with friends who'd felt betrayed when she'd disappeared without a word.

Other changes had been a blessing, though. She had moved into Nolan's house to take care of him and was still living there. Their relationship continued to mend and they were closer than they had ever been. Her veterinary license had been reinstated. Enigma's business had grown significantly, giving Griffin all the work he wanted.

He propped the metal spatula on the edge of the nearest platter and looked around. People laughed and talked, some in large groups, some in small. Several teens played volleyball behind the barn. "We've got a pretty good life."

She slipped her hand into his. "We do."

"Maybe we should change things up."

"What? Why would we want to do that?" She shook her head. "Things are good. I don't want anything to change."

He smiled down at her. "I thought you might be up for another name change."

"Name change?"

"This time to Devaney."

It took Laura a second to realize what he was asking. Her mouth dropped open. "Are you—?"

"Proposing? Yes, I am."

"Then yes!"

He snagged her waist and brought her to him for another kiss.

"I love that you did this here," she said. "I love *you*."

"The barn seemed the perfect place."

"It is."

Grinning, he looked over her head to the people beyond. "She said yes!"

A small smattering of applause broke out. She found her father still under the dogwood tree. He wore a pleased smile. As did Aunt Joy. Everyone was smiling and none of them looked surprised.

She tugged on the front of his T-shirt. "Did you plan this?"

"Sure did."

"You'd better be sure about that marriage

proposal, because Devaney is the name I plan to keep forever."

"That suits me just fine."

She laughed. "I can't believe you were able to keep this quiet."

"I'm pretty good at the undercover thing."

"No," she said softly. "You're the best."

* * * * *

Dear Reader,

Witness Undercover is a book I've wanted to write for several years. I'm thrilled to have the chance to tell the story of former navy SEAL Griffin Devaney and protected witness Laura Prentiss. When Laura comes out of hiding in order to save her desperately ill father, she is targeted for death by the former boyfriend she sent to prison. Griffin, now an operative for threat-management firm Enigma, Inc., is the man assigned to protect her. Filled with guilt over the deaths of his teammates, he is determined not to fail Laura the way he failed his friends and vows to guard her from the danger that is now threatening her. He never expected he would have to also guard his heart.

I hope you enjoyed meeting Griffin and Laura. I love hearing from readers and can be reached through email, Facebook or Twitter via my website: debracowan.net.

Happy Reading,
Debra Cowan

LARGER-PRINT BOOKS!

**GET 2 FREE
LARGER-PRINT NOVELS
PLUS 2 FREE
MYSTERY GIFTS**

Love Inspired®

Larger-print novels are now available...

YES! Please send me 2 FREE LARGER-PRINT Love Inspired® novels and my 2 FREE mystery gifts (gifts are worth about $10). After receiving them, if I don't wish to receive any more books, I can return the shipping statement marked "cancel." If I don't cancel, I will receive 6 brand-new novels every month and be billed just $5.49 per book in the U.S. or $5.99 per book in Canada. That's a savings of at least 19% off the cover price. It's quite a bargain! Shipping and handling is just 50¢ per book in the U.S. and 75¢ per book in Canada.* I understand that accepting the 2 free books and gifts places me under no obligation to buy anything. I can always return a shipment and cancel at any time. Even if I never buy another book, the two free books and gifts are mine to keep forever.

122/322 IDN GH6D

Name	(PLEASE PRINT)
Address	Apt. #
City	State/Prov.	Zip/Postal Code

Signature (if under 18, a parent or guardian must sign)

Mail to the **Reader Service:**
IN U.S.A.: P.O. Box 1867, Buffalo, NY 14240-1867
IN CANADA: P.O. Box 609, Fort Erie, Ontario L2A 5X3

**Are you a current subscriber to Love Inspired® books
and want to receive the larger-print edition?
Call 1-800-873-8635 or visit www.ReaderService.com.**

* Terms and prices subject to change without notice. Prices do not include applicable taxes. Sales tax applicable in N.Y. Canadian residents will be charged applicable taxes. Offer not valid in Quebec. This offer is limited to one order per household. Not valid to current subscribers to Love Inspired Larger-Print books. All orders subject to credit approval. Credit or debit balances in a customer's account(s) may be offset by any other outstanding balance owed by or to the customer. Please allow 4 to 6 weeks for delivery. Offer available while quantities last.

Your Privacy—The Reader Service is committed to protecting your privacy. Our Privacy Policy is available online at www.ReaderService.com or upon request from the Reader Service.

We make a portion of our mailing list available to reputable third parties that offer products we believe may interest you. If you prefer that we not exchange your name with third parties, or if you wish to clarify or modify your communication preferences, please visit us at www.ReaderService.com/consumerschoice or write to us at Reader Service Preference Service, P.O. Box 9062, Buffalo, NY 14240-9062. Include your complete name and address.

LILP15